W9-AUD-072

"Why haven't you married and had a family if that's what you think life is all about, Allie?"

She was thoughtful for a moment. "I guess I've been waiting to fall in love with a man my soul could love."

He fell silent. What could he say? Her words completely disarmed him, and he couldn't bring himself to make light of her admission. Her sincerity was without question. She would never marry lightly, or hold back any of herself. The man who captured her heart would have to be someone worthy of that love. He swallowed hard. "You deserve the best, Allie. Don't settle for anything less."

Books by Leona Karr
Love Inspired
Rocky Mountain Miracle #131

LEONA KARR

A native of Colorado, the author has always been inspired by God's magnificence, and she delights in using mountain valleys, craggy cliffs and high, snow-tipped peaks as a setting for many of her books. She began writing professionally in 1980 and has enjoyed seeing more than thirty of her romance books in print. The theme of "love conquers all" is an important message in all her stories.

Even though Leona contracted polio the year before the vaccine was approved, the blessings in her life have been many. "Wheeling and dealing" from a wheelchair, she has helped raise four children, pursued a career as a reading specialist and recently, after being widowed for five years, found a new love and soul mate in her own "Love Inspired" marriage.

She strives to write stories that will enrich the spiritual lives of those who read them, and is grateful to the many readers who have found her books filled with warm, endearing characters like those in *Rocky Mountain Miracle*.

Rocky Mountain Miracle
Leona Karr

Published by Steeple Hill Books™

If you purchased this book without a cover you should be aware
that this book is stolen property. It was reported as "unsold and
destroyed" to the publisher, and neither the author nor the
publisher has received any payment for this "stripped book."

STEEPLE HILL BOOKS

ISBN 0-373-87138-4

ROCKY MOUNTAIN MIRACLE

Copyright © 2001 by Leona Karr

All rights reserved. Except for use in any review, the reproduction
or utilization of this work in whole or in part in any form by any
electronic, mechanical or other means, now known or hereafter
invented, including xerography, photocopying and recording, or in
any information storage or retrieval system, is forbidden without
the written permission of the editorial office, Steeple Hill Books,
300 East 42nd Street, New York, NY 10017 U.S.A.

All characters in this book have no existence outside the imagination of
the author and have no relation whatsoever to anyone bearing the same
name or names. They are not even distantly inspired by any individual
known or unknown to the author, and all incidents are pure invention.

This edition published by arrangement with Steeple Hill Books.

® and TM are trademarks of Steeple Hill Books, used under license.
Trademarks indicated with ® are registered in the United States Patent
and Trademark Office, the Canadian Trade Marks Office and in other
countries.

Visit us at www.steeplehill.com

Printed in U.S.A.

For I know the plans I have for you,
saith the Lord, plans for good and not for evil,
to give you a future and hope.

—Jeremiah 29:11

With love to my husband, Michael,
my friend, sweetheart and beloved soulmate

Chapter One

Thick stands of ponderosa pine trees hugged a narrow mountain road winding upward into the Colorado Rocky Mountains. Allie Lindsey's hands tightened on the steering wheel as her thoughts raced ahead.

A few miles more and she'd be meeting Scott Davidson again for the first time in nearly six years. When they were both in high school, the two of them had spent the summer as teenage counselors in a youth church camp, and Allie had had a crush on the good-looking young man. She smiled inwardly as she remembered an adolescent kiss that had sent her heart pounding on the last night at camp.

After that summer, Allie had lost track of Scott when he and his younger brother, Jimmy, quit coming to Colorado to spend summers with their divorced father, and instead remained in California with their mother. But now Scott was back. Allie gave her chin a determined lift and mentally braced herself for the confrontation with him that lay ahead. As she navigated the twisting road in her blue Chevy she went over in her mind once again the events of the day before.

"What do you mean, we have to cancel the church camp?" Allie had stared at the church secretary as if she'd suddenly taken leave of her senses. "You can't mean it, Harriet."

The older woman sighed, "I'm afraid so."

Allie couldn't believe what she was hearing. She'd stopped by the church to help with last minute preparations for the summer camp only ten days away. For months, the junior youth group had been raising money to spend two whole weeks in the Colorado Rockies at a place called Rainbow Camp. Anticipation was like a live wire sending sparks in every direction as twenty boys and girls, ages eight to twelve, prepared for the June camp.

Allie was a middle school counselor for Denver public schools, and she knew how important this outing was for some of the city kids. Although they lived in the shadow of the Rocky Mountains, most had never camped out beside a mountain brook, breathed pine-scented air or sang songs around a dancing campfire.

"We got this in the mail today." Harriet handed her a letter.

Allie's greenish-blue eyes widened in disbelief as she read it. Mr. Sam Davidson who owned the land and buildings that had been used by churches and charity groups for years had recently died. His son Scott was cancelling all summer reservations in lieu of making preparations for selling the mountain property. Allie remembered Scott's father, Sam Davidson, as a generous soul who was extremely patient with the hordes of young people who flowed in and out of his camp all summer.

"Apparently Mr. Davidson passed away several weeks ago but no one notified us," she added. "I guess the lawyers were waiting to see what his son was going to do. And now we know," Harriet said with a tightening of her lips. "I just talked to Reverend Hanson on the phone. He's out of town attending a regional conference in New Mexico, and won't be back until next weekend. He knows that at this late date there's no chance of finding other accommodations, so he says to break the news as gently as we can." Harriet looked at Allie hopefully. "Maybe you're the one to do it. I mean, with your background and all."

"Oh, sure." Allie shoved a long strand of honey-brown hair behind her ear. "I know exactly how to break a bunch of kids' hearts." She read the letter again, and then straightened her shoulders. "Well, I suppose it has to be done."

Breathing a prayer that she would handle the situation as well as possible under the circumstances, Allie walked slowly down the stairs to a full-length basement room used for all kinds of church activities.

As she approached the door, she could hear Lily Twesbury's voice enthusiastically describing various wildflowers to be seen in mountain meadows and along the riverbeds. "We'll have lots of fun hiking all over the place, and making our own nature books to bring back home.''

Some of the kids clapped and cheered, sending daggers straight into Allie's heart. As inconspicuously as she could, Allie slipped to the back of the room. As she stood there, looking at the circle of children sitting on the floor, her eyes settled on Randy Cleaver's dark head.

Randy was a ten-year-old boy who had been on the streets most of his life because of a home situation with alcoholic parents. Allie knew the boy from escapades that had sent the wiry little troublemaker to her counseling office at school. Randy was tough as nails. A real handful. Just recently he'd been put in a foster home with church-going guardians who thought that sending him to church camp might help straighten him out. Now that hope was down the drain.

She had been the one to convince the boy that he ought to give summer camp a try, but she wasn't sure he'd agreed for the right reasons. A city kid, raised in one of the toughest neighborhoods, Randy showed little appreciation for wildflowers and nature studies. But he'd been surprisingly cooperative when it came to washing cars in order to earn money for the outing. She hated to think how he might act out his disappointment.

Randy was sitting beside Cathy Crawford, a small eight-year-old girl with a mop of yellow curls. She had contracted meningitis when she was only four, and it had left her with a significant hearing impairment. Tiny for her age, she was terribly shy. She wasn't inclined to do much talking even when she was in a friendly group and understood what was going on. The little girl was so sheltered by her parents that she rarely made any decisions on her own. Allie really felt that Cathy needed this time away from her parents, and it had taken a great deal of coaxing on Allie's part to persuade her family that attending a summer camp would be a positive experience for their daughter. Now all of that effort was going to be wasted.

As soon as the last slide was shown, Trudy Daniels, a plump Sunday school teacher in her early twenties, came in with refreshments. "Here you go, gang." With squeals of delight the youngsters rushed toward the trays of cookies and drinks.

Allie's spirits sank lower just thinking about Trudy's reaction to the news that all of their work was for naught. The young woman was a spark plug in the youth program and had become Allie's good friend. They'd spent numberless hours seeing to a hundred details that two weeks in the mountains with twenty children and five chaperones entailed.

After Allie told her the news, Trudy sighed. "Well, I guess if it's God's will, we should accept it."

Allie stared at her and echoed, "God's will?" The words hung in the air. How could it be God's will? The Bible was full of praise for His wondrous creation of rivers, mountains and open sky. Why would the good Lord want to deprive these children of experiencing that heavenly wonder?

With inspirational insight, the answer came bright and clear. *He wouldn't!* It wasn't divine intervention standing in the way of these children enjoying God's out-of-doors—it was Scott Davidson.

Allie turned to Trudy, her eyes flashing. "I've got an idea. Reverend Hanson is going to be out of town for the next few days. Let's hold off saying anything to anyone about this until he gets back," she said, and then made a quick exit before her puzzled friend could ask any questions.

Hurrying upstairs, Allie made her way to the church office, and got Scott's number from Harriet.

Allie dialed the number, moistened her lips and was ready with her persuasive argument. But after a few rings, a recording kicked in.

The voice was one she remembered, and just hearing it threw her off balance for a moment. She gave a nervous laugh. "Hi, Scott. This is Allie Lindsey— a voice from your past. I'd like to talk with you about the cancellation of our church camp, and I'd appreciate it if you'd give me a call." She gave him her telephone number and then added, "Nice to hear your voice again."

After she hung up, Allie stared at the telephone for a long minute. A mixture of emotions she couldn't quite define made her uneasy. Maybe she shouldn't have told Scott why she was calling? Maybe she should have waited until he called back to tell him? No, better to be up front about it. He might think she was trying to renew a personal relationship with him. For all she knew he could have married in the six years since she'd seen him last.

"Well?" Harriet prodded.

Allie reined in her wayward thoughts and gave

Harriet a reassuring smile. "Don't say anything to anyone about the letter until I talk with him. Hopefully, he'll give me a call later today."

But he didn't.

Allie jumped every time the phone rang, but it was only someone wanting to clean her carpets, or soliciting donations. She spent a restless night, and by nine o'clock the next morning, Scott Davidson still hadn't returned her call.

With stubborn intent, she phoned him again, and got the same recording, but she could tell from the short signal that he'd picked up his earlier messages. That's when she made up her mind to confront him face-to-face. Rainbow Camp was only a couple of hours from Denver. If she left right away, she could get there a little before noon, and make it back by nightfall.

She took a moment to study her reflection in a mirror, trying to decide if Scott would find her terribly changed from the high school girl he'd kissed in the moonlight. Her slender figure was still in good condition from routine jogging and watching her diet. Her honey-brown hair had darkened slightly but it still had golden highlights and a soft natural curl that framed her face and highlighted her blue eyes. A summer sun had begun to touch her arms, legs and face with a warm tan.

Not movie star material, she thought as she playfully blew a kiss at her reflection. "But you'll do."

As she left the city behind and headed west into pine-covered hillsides, thick aspen groves and vaulting rocky cliffs, Allie realized how much she'd missed these mountains. She'd only returned to Colorado late in September, having left the state after graduating from high school in order to attend an eastern college where her parents had moved in their retirement. Allie had been born to them late in life, and after their deaths, she had accepted the middle school counselor's position in Denver because the memories of growing up here were warm and inviting.

Her six-year's absence faded as the miles sped by, and she was again filled with awe at God's magnificence as the narrow road climbed in a serpentine pattern over mountain passes and then dropped down into beautiful valleys where green meadows and white-foamed streams flowed in silvery ribbons. Sam Davidson had built his Rainbow Camp in one of these beautiful mountain canyons. The buildings of the camp were set along a mountain river fed by melting snow from glaciers in the high country.

As Allie turned off of the highway to follow a graveled road through the trees, her heart quickened with expectation. A narrow bridge built of weathered timbers crossed the fast moving stream, and when a familiar panorama of cabins and other buildings came into view, a nostalgic lump caught in her throat.

Picnic tables still nestled in the grove of lodgepole pines and white-trunked aspen. Inviting paths hugged the riverbank and skirted smooth huge boulders where one could sit for an idle moment or a few minutes of meditation. She wondered if Steller's jays still nested in the high ponderosa pines growing close to the recreation and cafeteria building. This was the beauty she wanted to share with Randy, Cathy and the other children.

The abandoned air of the camp mocked her mission. The cabins were closed. No woodpiles had been collected on the porches to feed the fireplaces. The larger buildings were dark and shuttered, and as her eyes anxiously traveled over the rustic three-storied log-and-rock house that had been Sam's home, she failed to see any sign that it was occupied. She had assumed because Scott's voice was on the telephone answering machine that he must be staying here.

She forced herself to ignore a rising sense of frustration as she parked in a wide clearing in front of the main house, and let the car door shut with a bang that echoed her uneasiness.

As she hurried up a flight of wooden stairs leading up to a veranda porch that skirted the front of the log house, she thought she saw a flicker of movement behind the large front window. Her breathing quickened.

So someone was here!

The front door opened before she reached it. As he stood just inside, filling up the doorway, she let out her breath in giddy relief. "Scott, you're here! I was beginning to think that I'd made the trip for nothing." When he didn't answer, she said quickly, "I hope you don't mind...my coming like this?"

She knew nervousness was making her talk too fast, but the man standing there staring at her was not the Scott Davidson she remembered at all. Instead of soft lips easing into a boyish smile, his mouth was held in a firm line and his unsmiling grayish-green eyes narrowed. His dark hair no longer drifted in unruly waves around his face but was precisely layered in a short, fashionable cut that matched his expensive slacks and monogrammed sports shirt.

When his frown was her only answer, she added pointedly, "It's important that I speak with you."

Allie felt a rising sense of defeat just looking at him. This was a stranger who eyed her with obvious annoyance. *What has happened to you, Scott?* She firmed her chin. "When you didn't return my call I decided to drive up and see you."

His expression didn't change. "I'm trying to get everything taken care of in a few days and get back to my brokerage business. I'm sorry, but I haven't had time to return all my calls," he added in way of apology, but there was no warmth in his voice. "You said on the phone that you wanted to talk about the cancellation of a church camp. I'm afraid you've made the trip for nothing, Allie. The property is already in the hands of the Realtor, and I've had several offers on it already."

"I understand, but surely you can spare a few minutes to talk about it," she said pointedly, determined that he wasn't going to turn her away from her mission so easily.

A hint of a smile touched his lips. "Still got that streak of dogged stubbornness, I see. All right, come in, and we'll talk. I have to admit that when I got your message, I thought about that optimistic nature of yours, Allie, and wondered if you were still looking at life as some kind of a great adventure."

"You were pretty much of an optimist, yourself," she reminded him.

He didn't answer as he waved her into the living room that seemed unchanged to Allie after all these years. The same Indian rug was spread in front of the fireplace, and the lingering tobacco scent of Sam's pipe still mingled with an aromatic residue of pine log fires that had warmed chilly evenings for many years. Small tables and wall shelves held bits of driftwood, polished rocks from the riverbed, dried wildflowers and other treasures that Sam had brought in from the outdoors. The same Western pictures hung on the wall, and Sam's old scarred upright piano stood in the corner with its wobbly piano bench. Allie remembered the evenings some of the young campers had collected around the old piano, singing a rollicking tune or quiet hymn. As before, a couple of lumpy couches faced each other in a conversational grouping near the large front window.

Scott must have been sitting there when she drove up because there were papers scattered on one of the cushions. He motioned for her to sit down on the clean couch while he scooted papers into a pile on the other one. "Would you like a cup of coffee? I'm afraid that's all I have to offer."

"No, thanks, I'm fine." Her stomach was much too tight to even think about drinking or eating. "I'm truly sorry about your father," she said, seeking neutral ground for the moment. "He was a wonderful man."

Allie was taken back by the emptiness in Scott's reply. "In some ways he was, and in other ways he was a fool. He lived from hand to mouth, barely managed to pay the taxes, let alone keep the place up the way he should have. Dad had dozens of opportunities to sell the property because of the nearby ski resorts, but, no, he turned them all down.'' Scott ran agitated fingers through his raven hair. ''Stubborn. Pigheaded. Wouldn't listen to anyone. I begged him to come to California with me. I've done well with my investments. He didn't have to die here alone, almost penniless.''

''But your father loved this place,'' she protested. ''And he gave of himself to many young people whose lives were changed because of him. He was rich in ways that really matter.''

Scott stared at her for a long moment, and then said sadly, ''You haven't grown up at all, have you, Allie? I can tell that you're still caught up in the illusion that depriving yourself of all the good things in life is akin to holiness.''

''It would depend upon your definition of good things.''

The ring of a telephone in the hall stopped him from answering, and brought him to his feet. ''Excuse me,'' he said, ''I'm expecting a call.'' He disappeared through the doorway.

She heard him answer the phone and say, ''No, Mother, it's all right, things are moving slower than I expected.''

Allie had never met Scott's mother, Madeline. The Davidsons were divorced when both sons were small, but from the things Scott and Jimmy had said about their mom, Madeline was a no-nonsense, worldly businesswoman. Allie could tell from Scott's end of the telephone that he was being pressured to leave the property in the hands of a Realtor and come back to California. She wondered where Jimmy was, and if he was as eager to get rid of the property as Scott and his mother were. He wasn't wearing a wedding ring so there must not be any Mrs. Scott Davidson.

While waiting for him to finish his telephone conversation, Allie got up from the couch and idly walked over to one of the bookcases. Drawing out a couple of photo albums that caught her eye, she remembered that Scott's father loved to take pictures with his small camera.

Sitting back down on the couch, Allie started thumbing through one of the albums. She smiled at photos of a boyish Scott and grinning Jimmy as the boys grew with each summer visit. Three years younger than Scott, Jimmy idolized his older brother and Allie chuckled seeing their grinning faces as they held up a prize fish, or showed off by walking across the river on a fallen log.

In the second album, she found some pictures taken the summer when she and Scott were teenage counselors at the church camp. Glowing-faced young people she'd forgotten were pictured eating hot dogs, or squealing as they dipped their feet into the white-foamed stream. She quietly laughed at a photo of herself sitting on a log, her shoulder-length blond hair flying in every direction and her bare legs dangling in the water. There were a couple of photos of her and Scott walking hand in hand, and she remembered the midnight walk with Scott that ended with her first romantic embrace and kiss.

How simple and wonderful life had been that halcyon summer, she thought, looking at a picture of the two of them taken the summer when they were seventeen. Then they'd gone their separate ways, and lost track of each other. Now their paths had crossed again, but she felt as distant from Scott Davidson as she would have with a stranger.

Closing the albums, she steeled herself for what lay ahead. Seeing the old Scott, smiling and carefree in the photos gave her the courage she needed to ignore his distant, cold manner. When he hung up the hall phone and came back into the room, she laughed and said, "Look what I found."

"Dad's old photos?"

Impulsively, she reached up, grabbed his hand, pulled him down on the couch beside her. Maybe, just maybe, he might be touched by the memories of the wonderful summers he'd spent in Colorado with his father.

Scott stiffened against her nearness as she sat close to him, turning the pages of the album. He didn't need any old photos to remember the way her face glowed with animation and laughter, nor the way her supple body had felt as she walked hand in hand beside him in the moonlight. His first love had changed little in six years. Her honey-gold hair still glinted with highlights, and a touch of lipstick defined the sweet curve of her lips. Her lavender-blue eyes as soft as a summer sky still radiated an innocent warmth. How foolishly naive they'd been that summer between high school and college. Their childish faith had seemed enough to slay dragons, but the world had been waiting with its unrelenting harsh reality, and they hadn't even known it.

Aware of his gaze traveling over her face, Allie suddenly felt self-conscious. What was he thinking? Was he remembering the kiss he'd given her, and his promise to keep in touch? They'd been separated by a whole continent when he went to college in California, and she attended an eastern university. Life had spun off in different directions for both of them, and even before the end of their freshman year they had lost touch with each other. Now, for the first time since she'd arrived, he seemed to be aware of her as a person.

Laughing softly, she pointed to a photo taken on skit night at camp when everyone dressed in costume. There they were in the front row, Scott as Robin Hood, and she was Maid Marian. Jimmy stood next to Scott, a pillow stuffed in his pants, playing chubby Friar Tuck. Jimmy had made up a corny skit about Sherwood Forest. The boys had run around, pretending to use bows and arrows while rescuing Maid Marian from the castle.

Allie glanced at Scott's face, expecting a brief smile, but his expression was as tight and full of pain as any she'd ever seen. Stunned by his response to the photo, she stammered, "What...what is it?"

He turned hard eyes on her. "You don't know?"

"Know what?"

"You don't know about Jimmy?"

Her mouth was suddenly as parched as a desert.

Living with her parents in the east and going to college there had cut her off from any of her Colorado contacts, and since she'd been back at the start of the school year, she hadn't heard anything of the Davidsons until the church letter from Scott. "What is it? What happened?"

She saw him clench his hands so tightly that the veins stood up like purple chords. "He was murdered."

"Murdered," she echoed, cursing herself for not knowing. *Oh, dear God, why hadn't someone told her?*

"Two years ago." He drew in a deep breath, trying to control the raging anger that was still there. "Jimmy was killed in a street fight that broke out during a demonstration against drug houses."

"Oh, I'm so sorry. I didn't know."

Scott's lips twisted bitterly. "If it hadn't been for me, my brother wouldn't have been killed that night."

"You can't blame yourself for something that was out of your control."

"Oh, it was under my control, all right. When some Christian young people from various churches were trying to get a handle on some of the street gangs, I talked Jimmy into helping. He always did what I wanted him to do, and was my shadow growing up. My mother kept telling me whatever happened to him would be on my conscience. She was right. It should have been me, not Jimmy, who died in the streets."

"But you couldn't have known what was going to happen." Allie tried to take his hand but he jerked it away.

"I decided not to go on the demonstration because I had a religious seminar that night, but Jimmy went. If God wasn't going to protect him that night, I should have been there, watching out for him. Instead of wasting my time listening to someone preach about God's goodness."

"God *is* good. Jimmy was a victim of the free choice between good or evil that all people have—why blame God?"

"Because the shape the world's in is proof enough for me that God is an absentee Lord. I'm through believing that there's a divine power interested in me or anyone else. Someone else can carry the banner high—and get killed for it. Not me."

"Aren't you being a little self-indulgent?"

His jaw tightened. "Save your Sunday school lectures, Allie. I've heard them all before."

She searched for some way to help him through the guilt that was obviously eating him alive, but her master's degree in counseling seemed totally inadequate in the face of his bitterness. Not only had he changed on the outside, but a loss of faith was like a malignancy eating away at his soul.

He stood up. "I'm sorry you made the trip for nothing, Allie. Now, if you'll excuse me, I have to get back to working on a hundred details that have to be cleared up before the property sells. You can see for yourself how impossible it would be to get the camp in any kind of shape in less than two weeks."

She grabbed the objection like a fish to a hook. "That wouldn't be a problem. I know we could get a working crew from the church to come up and put the place in order.''

"I don't have time to oversee—"

"I do,'' she said brightly, standing up and facing him. "I'm on my summer break from my school counselor's job. You could leave everything to me and go about your business getting ready to sell the place. You see, there's this little boy, Randy Cleaver. He's been on the streets most of his life because of alcoholic parents and there's a little girl who's losing her hearing—"

"Save it, Allie. I told you I'm way past trying to fix the ills of the world."

"I know.'' She paused, searching for guidance, and suddenly divine inspiration like a heavenly butterfly flitted through her thoughts. She knew exactly what approach she should use to touch his conscience. "I was really thinking about Jimmy and your dad. This place has always been special to them.''

"What are you getting at?''

"Even now, Rainbow Camp really belongs as much to your father and brother as it does to you, doesn't it? If Sam and Jimmy were here, I don't think they'd disappoint a bunch of kids who have their hearts set on coming to summer camp.''

"But Dad and Jimmy aren't here, are they?''

"I believe they are, in spirit, and you know what they would want you to do,'' she countered.

Of course he knew. Anger built up in Scott that he was the one who had been left to deal with the past.

Abruptly he walked away from her, and as he let his gaze travel around the room, his heart tightened.

Jimmy's worn baseball glove lay on the shelf where Allie had removed the photo albums, and in a nearby corner of the room stood several fishing rods where his dad had left them.

Scott put his hand on the mantel of the fireplace, and bent his head as his ears were suddenly filled with remembered sounds; his dad thumping out a hymn on the old piano, and Jimmy's boyish voice on the stairs. His shoulders went slack.

You know what they would want you to do.

Finally, he lifted his head, turned around, and looked at Allie with those intense eyes of his. She drew in a prayerful breath as she waited for him to speak.

Please, God.

"All right, Allie. You win," he said in a thick voice of surrender. "In memory of Dad and Jimmy, you can have your church camp one more time."

"Thank you."

She could have hugged him in joyful relief, but he was already walking toward the door, opening it, as if anxious to have her gone.

Chapter Two

Why did you agree to her request? Scott asked himself as he endeavored to put his thoughts in order after a restless night.

His time plan for turning the property over to a Realtor for immediate listing had been ambushed by a blue-eyed charmer from his past. When he'd heard Allie Lindsey's voice on his answering machine, he'd felt an undefinable quiver of excitement, but as soon as she had stated her business, the joy had died. The few days he'd spent in the old house had been trying enough, but enduring a two-week church camp would only create a situation that he'd been trying to avoid. The last thing he wanted to do was to surround himself with a past that had promised so much, and delivered only heart-wrenching disappointment.

The camp was, also, far from being ready for twenty kids and their chaperones. His father's death six weeks ago had put an end to any preparations for the summer. Scott had been slow in picking up the reins and canceling reservations because his father had not kept any kind of organized records. Fortunately, the Irish couple, Patrick and Dorie O'Toole, who worked for his dad had filled him in on the summer schedule.

The O'Tooles had helped Sam run the camp for more than fifteen years. They'd been friends with Scott since he was eleven years old, and all the summers that he and Jimmy had spent in Colorado, the couple had been almost family. The boys had spent lots of nights at their house, listening to Patrick play the guitar, and eating Dorie's good cooking whenever they got the chance. Patrick was a raw-bone handyman who did everything from handling the camp's maintenance to supervising exuberant youngsters during the summer and playing a mean game of chess with Sam. His chubby, outgoing wife, Dorie, ran the camp dining room, and her plump figure was a testimonial to her own cooking. She always had a ready hug and smile, and having children around her seemed to make up for the lack of her own. Scott knew how much his dad depended upon the O'Tooles to keep things in the camp running smoothly.

A sense of urgency suddenly overtook Scott. Right after the funeral, Scott had told them that he was closing down the camp and selling the property. They seemed to understand that it was the only thing he could do. Property values were at a premium in this mountain area because of the developing ski areas close by.

What if Pat and Dorie had already sold their own house across the river and moved away? *How on earth will I get the camp ready by myself?* he asked himself with a start. The last time he'd seen them at the funeral, the grief in their eyes and the slump of their shoulders had told him how much they loved his father. With so many other things on his mind, Scott hadn't given them a thought—until now. With a jolt, he realized that he hadn't seen either of them in the few days that he'd been back.

Throwing back the bed covers, he slipped into a pair of cords and a sportsman's pullover. A valiant sun was breaking through the low, misty clouds as he left the house, and the promise of a lovely June day was in the offing. Breathing in deeply the high mountain air, he drew in pungent smells of pine resin and tangy cedar. He'd almost forgotten how beautifully clear and fresh everything looked with the sparkle of sunshine deepening nature's tapestries. His ears were filled with the sound of rushing waters lapping and sucking over rocks in the swift-flowing river, and he remembered early morning fishing treks with his dad along the banks. They'd catch their breakfast, and the taste of fresh rainbow trout cooked in butter would always linger in his memory. He'd tried ordering trout in fancy Los Angeles restaurants, but the meal had always been a disappointment.

Just like life, he thought, and he stiffened against memories that taunted him. He should have handled everything through a Realtor. Coming back was a mistake, a big mistake.

He broke into an easy run and his footsteps echoed on the planked bridge as he crossed the river. Patrick and Dorie's log house was built on the side of a hill on the opposite side of the river from the camp. He bounded up the roughly hewn steps, and knocked briskly on the thick pine door. Homemade chimes hanging from a porch rafter moved in the early morning breeze, making sounds like the muffled notes of an organ.

"Well, saints preserve us, look who's here," Dorie said, wiping her hands on her voluminous apron as she opened the door. "We were thinking that you were still in Californy."

"I've been back a few days. I'm trying to go through some things at the house." He knew his excuse was lame for not coming by and seeing them.

"Pat! Pat, we got company," she called to her husband. Then she winked at Scott. "Sure, and I knew there was some reason for making a batch of buttermilk pancakes. It isn't every day a handsome fellow comes calling."

"You must have heard my stomach growling all the way here," he teased back, his spirits suddenly made lighter by her laughter. He remembered all the times that he'd found comfort in her good humor. More than once through the years she'd put loving arms around a lonely boy who missed his mother. She'd never met Madeline Davidson, but Scott could tell Dorie didn't hold much with a mother who could be away from her sons three months out of the year.

"Come on to the kitchen," she said, leading the way.

Patrick was sitting at the kitchen table drinking a mug of coffee. He was a lanky fellow with a short, reddish beard that covered his bony chin, and a thatch of sandy-colored hair that never wanted to smooth down. There was a surprised lift to his eyebrows as he looked at Scott, but his expression wasn't friendly like his wife's. "We didn't expect to see you in these parts again," he said gruffly.

Patrick's briskness made it clear that he didn't look upon a visit from Scott as a cause for celebration. "What you come over for? Need some help tearing down the place? Can't them high-flying land speculators bring in their own crews?"

The gravel in his voice warned Scott that he'd put himself in the enemy camp by deciding to sell out to investors. He knew that Pat was like a lot of people who had homes in the canyon. For years they'd fought to keep out any kind of modern developments. They didn't like progress or change, and his father had been one of them.

"Now, Patrick," Dorie said with a warning shake of her pancake ladle—she always called him by his full name when she was irritated with him. "Don't you badger Scott. He's just trying to do the right thing."

"I'm here because I need yours and Dorie's help," Scott said frankly. He knew better than to try and out-fox the Irishman. As plainly as he could, he told them about his visit from Allie Lindsey.

"Oh, that's the pretty little lass that you took up with one summer," Dorie said eagerly. "I remember her."

Scott ignored the speculative look in her eyes. "We haven't been in touch for years. Anyway, I wrote a letter canceling her church's camp reservation, and

Allie came to see me, hoping to talk me into honoring Dad's commitment.''

"Oh, my," Dorie said, a frown creasing her round face.

"You can see the difficulty." Scott looked Pat straight in the eyes. "The cabins aren't ready. The buildings need all kinds of cleaning. I frankly don't see how we could get the place ready in a week, do you?" Somehow he knew he shouldn't tell the Irishman that he'd already committed himself.

Pat took a slow sip of coffee from his mug without giving Scott any indication that he had even heard what Scott had been saying. Then he turned to look at Scott, and he said in a non-committal tone. "I reckon it could be done."

"Sure it could," Dorie jumped in eagerly. "All the bedding is clean and ready. Glory, I could make a list of things we need in the shake of a cat's tail."

"What do you think, Pat?" Scott asked in a deferential manner. They all knew that the decision rested with him. Dorie was wife enough not to push him, and Scott knew better than to pressure him.

Pat leaned back in his chair, his broad forehead creased in a thoughtful expression. "I reckon me and Dorie could handle things all right. I don't hold with the idea of disappointing a bunch of young 'uns."

Scott felt a heavy weight roll off of him. "I appreciate it, Patrick." Now, he could leave the whole camping thing in good hands and tend to his own business.

Dorie beamed. "It's funny how the good Lord works things out, isn't it? You and Allie together again after all these years. Such a cute couple, you were.''

Scott said rather shortly, "Don't try and play Cupid, Dorie. I doubt that we'll even see much of each other." He could have said that he had no intention of interacting with the church group. As far as Allie was concerned, he'd already told her how he felt about her strong religious convictions. He knew that she disapproved of his worldly lifestyle and anti-religious convictions. "We have nothing in common anymore."

"It's Jimmy's death, isn't it?" Dorie said gently. "Sure and I can see why your heart's broken. T'was a horrible thing to have happened." Then she touched his arm with her gentle hand, and said softly, "Your father grieved over the loss of his son, but it didn't destroy his faith in God."

"I'm not my father," Scott said firmly.

Patrick nodded. "No, you're not, more's the pity, lad."

He left their house, knowing it was true—you can't go home again. Too many things change.

When Allie and Trudy arrived at the camp early in the morning a few days later, Allie couldn't believe how different it looked from her first visit. There was a hint of expectancy all over the place. A grocery delivery truck was parked at a side kitchen door, some of the cabins were open and a load of wood had been dumped nearby, waiting to be distributed among the buildings.

Scott had called her, reporting that the O'Tooles

had agreed to take charge and get the camp ready. He told her that an extra pair of hands or two would be appreciated, but he was emphatic about not needing an invasion of church people. "They'll just be in the way," he said ungraciously.

"Okay," she responded without further comment, relieved that he hadn't found some way to back out of their agreement. "If it's all right with you, my friend, Trudy, and I will come up for a couple of days and see how we can help out."

"Good. Doric will appreciate the extra hands."

"It'll be nice to see the O'Tooles again. I remember them as a very nice couple who really enjoyed having all of us around."

"Dorie remembers you, too," he admitted but omitted in what context.

"Don't you remember the picnic box Dorie fixed for us the day we decided to hike up to the top of Redridge?"

"I remember," he answered flatly. "See you in a couple of days."

Such enthusiasm, she thought as she hung up. He obviously didn't intend to engage in any watercolor memories of "the way we were." Fine. He could chill out all he wanted, she decided with a spurt of pride— or was it disappointment? All she cared about was making sure the kids had a wonderful outing. Anyway, she doubted that Scott would stick around for the whole time, unless making arrangements for selling the property kept him at the camp.

"I can hardly wait to meet this ogre," Trudy confessed as they drove into the camp. "He sounds like a real loser."

"Oh, Scott's not really all that bad," Allie said quickly, surprised that she was so ready to defend him. "I told you what happened to his brother. Scott's carrying around a heavy load of guilt, and I suspect his mother isn't helping much."

"Uh-huh." Trudy's tone was noncommittal. She'd lost a young husband in a car accident when a drunk driver plowed into them one evening after church services. Instead of blaming God and giving up, Trudy had used her anger to help in the campaign against drinking and driving.

"Don't rock the boat, Trudy," Allie warned as she stopped the car in front of the old house. "Scott agreed to let us have our camp, and that's all that matters. Don't be attacking him. We really don't know what happened and what kind of wounds need healing under that crisp veneer of his."

Trudy studied her friend's flushed face, and let out a slow whistle. "Are you still carrying something around for this fellow?"

"Of course not," Allie said quickly. Maybe too quickly, she told herself, wondering why the question made her feel defensive. Why was she letting Trudy bait her? "We haven't seen each other for years. And the last time we were together we were just teenagers."

"Some first loves are deep enough to last a lifetime," Trudy warned.

"I wouldn't think a little hand-holding, and one

adolescent kiss in the moonlight could be called a deep first love.''

"But you haven't forgotten him.''

"No, I suppose I haven't. But at the time, I was naive enough to believe that Scott and I were soul mates. I guess that's why I felt differently about him from all of the other fellows I'd dated at that time.''

"Okay, a word of warning from an older and wiser woman—''

"You're a year older than I am,'' laughed Allie.

"Right. Heed your elders. Don't tear yourself up because the young boy who kissed you in the moonlight is now a man who has turned against himself and God. Just remember, Allie, life has a way of giving us lessons that we need, and Scott Davidson may be in for more than his share.''

"It's so sad that he's lost his dad and his brother. The place must be filled with painful memories for him,'' Allie lamented as they got out of the car and walked up the steps of the house. In spite of herself, she felt a faint flicker of apprehension as they waited for him to answer their knock.

No sign of life at the windows. Allie tried to deny a wave of disappointment when it was obvious that he wasn't there and wasn't going to open the door. Maybe he'd already locked up the house, turned the camp over to the O'Tooles and gone back to California.

"Let's check in at the dining hall. I bet Dorie has a bunch of chores lined up for us to tackle.''

A row of cabins stretched along the river, and an L-shaped dormitory stood next to a large building that was divided into the dining hall and activity room. Allie could see that even though Sam had tried to keep up with needed repairs, all of the buildings were showing the effects of time.

"See that stand of huge spruce trees?" Allie pointed ahead. "Right in the middle of them, there's a natural grouping of rocks around an open space that makes a wonderful setting for early-morning worship services. It's great for private meditation too, although my favorite spot is a large boulder just around the bend of the river."

She drew in a deep breath of pine-scented air, and time sped backward to the wonderful hours she'd spent walking through the trees and listening to the musical roar of the rushing stream.

"You love this place, don't you?" Trudy said with a smile.

Allie nodded, "I didn't realize how much I really do. I can hardly wait to walk some of the old trails and check out some of my favorite spots along the river."

"Well, I'm glad we've got a good cook," Trudy said. "The outdoors always makes me ravenous." She stuck her hands in her ample overalls. It was clear that having lots of good food for a healthy appetite was the most important thing as far as Trudy was concerned.

"Hiking over some of these hills will give you an appetite, all right."

"Hiking?" Trudy mimicked. "Who said anything about hiking?"

Allie laughed as they mounted the steps to the dining room, and then sobered as the door flew open and Scott came out.

"Oh," she said with a start of surprise. "I thought you weren't here. I mean, we stopped at the house and I was thinking that you might have left the O'Tooles in charge, and locked up the house, and—" she caught herself. *Quit babbling.* What was there about him that flustered her so much that she sounded like a ninny?

"I'm still here, obviously."

"Yes, obviously," she said collecting herself. "This is my friend, Trudy Daniels."

"Nice to meet you, Trudy," Scott said politely.

"And you," Trudy responded with a smug smile. Allie could tell that Scott didn't look like anything Trudy had imagined. He wore jeans and a tight knit shirt that molded his well-conditioned muscles, and a deep tan testified to hours on the beach or on the water, and skiing. The veiled look she sent Allie, said, "Wow!"

"Wouldn't have missed it, Mr. Davidson."

"Scott," he corrected.

Trudy cocked her head and studied him with her large guileless eyes. "I have a feeling this will turn out to be the best outing our church kids ever had."

Allie hid a smile. Leave it to Trudy to put a positive spin on his reluctance to have them here.

"I hope that's the case, but we're playing catch-up," Scott answered honestly. "I'm really depending upon Pat and Dorie to run things." At that moment a sleek Mercedes came into view on the river bridge. Scott frowned as he looked at his watch. "I guess hauling in that load of firewood took me longer than I imagined. I've got some business appointments that will keep me busy. Why don't you check with the O'Tooles and see what needs to be done? Please excuse me."

With a thin smile, he brushed by them, and strode quickly toward the house where two men in business suits were getting out of their car.

"So that's the heartthrob," mused Trudy. "He's got a way about him, all right. No wonder you're having trouble closing the book on young love."

"I told you, we enjoyed an adolescent friendship for one summer. That's all, for heaven's sake. Will you quit trying to make it into some Romeo and Juliet drama?"

"I will, if you will."

"What?"

Trudy laughed. "I'm betting that the shiny flush on your face has nothing to do with the sun, nor is the high mountain air responsible for your quick breathing. You like this guy."

"Sure, I like him," admitted Allie. "At least, I used to, but that's water under the proverbial bridge. Scott's gone his way, and I've gone mine. Really, Trudy, I don't want to discuss it any further. We're here to help get things ready for the church camp. What Scott does or doesn't do isn't any concern of mine."

"Uh-huh," Trudy said.

"Let's go see what they have for us to do." She led the way into the dining room, and her breath caught as she looked around. The place looked as if a whirlwind had swept through it. Nothing was set up for the feeding of a crowd of hungry campers. Chairs were stacked, tables shoved together and all the counters loaded down with stacks of trays, cups and dishes. Only the floor looked bright and shiny from a recent scrubbing.

At that moment Dorie appeared in the kitchen doorway, "I thought I heard voices," she said as she greeted them with a merry wave of her hand from the kitchen. "Come on in. I'm busy putting away all the foodstuffs that have just been delivered."

"Can we help?"

"Sure." She looked as happy as a busy bee flitting around a field of clover. "I like to set up the kitchen myself." She nodded toward the connecting door between the dining room and the activity room. "I think Pat's been needing some help. Why don't you gals give a look-see?"

"Okay. We're here to do whatever needs doing."

"I'll let you know when I need an extra pair of hands," Dorie promised.

They left her happily humming to herself as she filled the freezer, fridge and cupboards. When they entered the recreation room, they saw that the same happy mood did not apply to her husband. Pat O'Toole was sitting on the edge of a raised dais that served as a stage, staring moodily around the room, as he filled his pipe.

"Oh, oh," murmured Allie. The recreation room was in a sorry state. All but one wall and the ceiling showed ugly watermarks around the windows and on the ceiling. Only one wall had been freshly painted a pretty rose color, and a heap of painting tarps and paint cans pushed to one side were evidence of an interrupted project.

Allie wasn't sure that Patrick O'Toole really remembered her. Unlike his wife, he had no welcoming smile on his lips nor recognition in his eyes as she introduced herself and Trudy. He just nodded at the introduction, and continued to give his attention to a pipe that he was trying to light.

"It's nice to see you again, Mr. O'Toole," Allie said brightly, ignoring his distant manner. "We're from the church. Just tell us what you want us to do. We're here to help."

He peered at her from under bushy eyebrows. "So you're the lass that talked Scott into keeping the camp open?"

"Yes, thank God," she said, relieved that he was speaking to her at least. "We appreciate your offer to handle everything for us."

"We've got some nice kids who are looking forward to coming to Rainbow Camp," Trudy said.

Patrick shook his head. "Well, ladies, I reckon I forgot how many things were left half-done after Sam's passing. Look at this room, would you?" He got up and walked around the room, pointing out the unpainted walls and ceiling. "We got all the leaks fixed and were starting to paint when Sam had his spell." He shook his head sadly, and Allie heard the break in his voice. "It's a disgrace to his memory to have anybody even see the place like this."

The two women exchanged glances, and Allie wasn't surprised when her friend spoke up. "Well then, Mr. O'Toole, I guess we'd better get to painting,'' Trudy told him in her take-charge manner. She eyed the ceiling. "A nice tall ladder will do just fine.'' In a few minutes she had organized the whole project. Allie knew that she was the one responsible for redecorating all the Sunday school rooms. Trudy could wield a paintbrush roller with the best of them.

The room was rather long and narrow, and even though one of the longer walls had already been done, the challenge of painting the other three and the ceiling kept them busy through the morning.

When Dorie brought in some drinks and sandwiches, they took a brief break for lunch. She nodded her approval. "Sam picked out that color. Said it reminded him of that cluster of moss roses down by the spring.''

Pat sighed. "I was telling him, the color would show hand prints to beat the band, but he didn't care. Crazy guy.'' He turned his head away quickly as if there were something in his eye.

They had to push to finish by late afternoon, but a sense of satisfaction made their effort worthwhile. They took a few minutes to enjoy their work as soft sunlight bathed the walls in a warm glow. It had certainly been satisfying.

"Nice work, ladies,'' Patrick said with a smile. "Sure and you're a credit to the Painters' Union.'' He winked at Trudy. "If I weren't a married man, I'd be giving you the eye, lass. I've got a few rooms at the house that could use your touch.''

They were all weary, but pleased with the job they'd done. Patrick started carrying out empty paint cans, and painting debris to the trash while Allie and Trudy put the room to rights.

"I'll ask Dorie for some cleaning rags," Trudy said, and headed for the kitchen.

A moment later, while Allie was putting some lids on some leftover paint cans, Scott came in the rec room. He took one look around at the freshly painted room with an expression of utter disbelief on his face.

Allie stood up, brushed back her hair, suddenly aware of the paint spatters on her arms, jeans and shirt. She looked a mess, but then, what did it matter? She smiled. "Looks nice, doesn't it?"

For a moment, he looked speechless. Then he swore, "What in blazes! Why on earth did you put in all this work, painting this room?"

She looked at him, stunned and dumbfounded. What was he so angry about?

"Is this some kind of subtle trick you're playing?" he lashed out.

"Trick?"

"Whatever you're trying to pull off, it won't work," he warred her. "You can't make me change my mind, Allie."

"I'm not trying to make you change your mind."

"Good, because I've just made arrangements for this building to be pulled down in three weeks."

Chapter Three

Scott struggled against a wave of exasperation. He was caught between trying to get things ready for the campers, while at the same time initiating a schedule to level the area and clear the property for potential buyers. Agreeing to open the camp had been a bad idea in the beginning, and it was getting worse by the minute.

Allie looked exhausted, tense and angry with him for challenging the decision to paint the room. On the defensive, he said, "I wished you'd asked me about it before putting in all this work."

With a determined lift to her head, she replied firmly, "It was important to Pat that we finish the job your father started before he died. Patrick knew Sam wouldn't want people in here with rain-stained walls even if this is the last time the room is to be used."

Scott silently fumed. It was just like her and Patrick to bring his father into the matter. They'd made their feelings clear enough, but it was the height of folly for them to spruce up the place. "Well, what's done is done."

In a moment of weighted silence that followed, Trudy came in with a broom and cleaning rags, and seeing Scott, started bragging about the job they'd done.

"Are we painters, or are we painters?" she challenged, grinning. "I just may give up my job working in my dad's restaurant, and find me a new career."

Her light banter fell flat. Allie's posture was stiff, and tension radiated from her jutting chin. Scott avoided eye contact with both of the women.

When neither Allie nor Scott returned Trudy's smile, her expression changed to one of puzzlement. "What gives? Did I miss something?"

"I'll tell you later," Allie said. She reached out and took the broom from Trudy, and started sweeping. "As soon as we get this room cleaned up, we ought to check out one of the cabins and get settled. I don't suppose it matters which one."

"I think the first cabin is ready. I just checked to make sure you had bedding and firewood," Scott said crisply. He ignored Allie, who had her back to him as she swept the floor. He recognized a cold shoulder when he got one, and directed his comments to Trudy. "I think everything's in order for the couple of nights you'll be here."

"Thanks," Trudy answered. "We'll be ready for a hot bath, won't we, Allie?" A slight nod was all she got as Allie gave her attention to picking up some drop cloths.

"I'd invite you to put up at the house, but it's a

mess,'' Scott said in an apologetic tone. ''I'm trying to get everything sorted and moved out. I don't think Dad threw away anything all the years he'd been here. He's got so much worthless stuff packed away that I'm tempted to just bag and dump it.''

''That must be a challenge,'' Trudy said sympathetically, doing her best to keep the conversation moving along compatible lines. ''I'd sure hate to have the job of cleaning out my folk's house. Every cupboard and closet is packed with stuff.''

''I've arranged for some book buyers, and second-hand store people to look things over. What they don't take, I'll have to haul away.'' Scott wished he could just walk away from the whole thing. Maybe his mother was right. He should have stayed in California and handled everything long distance. Too late now, he chided himself. His hands were tied for another two weeks. He owed it to Pat and Dorie to stick around until the church camp was over.

''I love old stuff,'' Trudy told him. Her large brown eyes sparkled. ''Can I have a look-see before you get rid of all of it?''

Scott looked surprised. ''Sure, be my guest. I have to warn you that most of the stuff is worn-out and wasn't worth much when it was new.''

''You never can tell,'' Trudy said with her usual optimism. ''There might be a treasure amidst all the junk.''

''If there is, you're welcome to it.'' He gave one last look around at the newly painted room, and managed to say, ''You ladies did a nice job.'' *Even if it was a stupid thing to do.*

After he'd gone, Allie explained the situation to Trudy. "This building is going to be torn down with the rest of the camp in three weeks. Scott couldn't believe we'd gone to all the work to paint it." She shook her head, every bone in her body protesting the day of hard labor. "I can't believe it, either."

"Hey, some things aren't suppose to last forever. You just have to enjoy them while you can, and then let them go." Trudy tipped back her dark head and surveyed the rose-colored walls. "It's enough that for three more weeks this is going to be the prettiest room in camp."

Allie smiled at her. "How'd you get so smart?"

"Oh, it just comes naturally," she answered flippantly. "I'm not just a pretty face, you know."

As they laughed together, Allie's spirits rose, and by the time they'd put the activity room in order, she'd felt a new rush of energy. "Let's move our stuff into the cabin, and see if the shower is working."

"It'd better be. I've got enough rose-colored spots on me to pass for a case of measles."

"Dorie's invited us over to their house for supper." Allie told her. "Their house is on the hillside across from the river. It's about a half-mile walk up a dirt road as I remember." Then she added with a smile, "Dorie said something about stuffed pork chops."

"Stuffed pork chops?" Trudy patted her rather ample hips. "I really shouldn't, but I've worked up an appetite with all this painting and cleaning." She eyed Allie's slim figure and sighed. "I bet you could eat twice as much as me, and never put on a pound."

"I wasn't raised around good cooking the way you

were," Allie said kindly. Trudy's folks owned a successful family restaurant, and since she was around food all the time, it was no wonder she had trouble keeping her weight down. "Come on, let's finish up here, and have a little time to put our feet up before dinner."

When they checked the first cabin, they saw that Scott had been true to his word. Fresh bedding was in a neat pile at the foot of two of the beds, clean towels in the bathroom and an automatic coffeepot ready to be plugged in. An electric wall heater had been turned on low, but what surprised them both was wood laid for a fire in the fireplace, just waiting for the touch of a match.

"I love a log fire," said Trudy as she plopped down on a rug, and lit the log kindling. When it was glowing, she stretched out full length in front of the fire, and closed her eyes. "I may have to change my mind about that guy." She opened one eye and peered at Allie. "Maybe you should give him a little slack."

"He's got all the slack he needs," Allie answered crisply as she got ready to take a shower.

"Hmm, sounds like there still may be a spark or two left between the two of you."

Allie answered evenly, "Don't try to play Cupid, Trudy. I don't even know this changed Scott Davidson, and we have absolutely nothing in common anymore. After the church camp, we probably will never see each other again." She gave a wry smile. "Of course, I may wring his neck long before then."

"Uh-huh," Trudy murmured. "You remember the old saying, don't you? Where there's smoke there's fire. Something between you two is still burning, I'm thinking.''

"Well, think again," Allie said curtly and went into the bathroom to take her shower. She was still fuming about the way Scott had lashed out at her. He was so blinded by his own selfish agenda that he couldn't even appreciate Patrick's feelings about the half-finished job Scott's dad had left. Allie usually was able to keep a firm rein on her temper, but she was ready to hold a mirror up to Scott Davidson, and let him take a look at the self-centered person he'd become.

When they were ready to go to dinner at the O'Tooles', Allie expected to drive the short distance, but Trudy said she'd better work off the pork chops before and after she ate them.

A lavender twilight was just settling in the canyon as heady pine-scented breezes still warm from the day's sun sent pale green aspen leaves quivering over their heads. As they walked across a narrow bridge spanning the river, rushing waters rose and fell over polished stones, creating a melody of gurgling sounds. Glimmers of silver shone like liquid ribbons in flowing waters darkening to purple in the approaching night.

They had just started up a narrow road cut into the side of the hill, when they heard an engine coming up behind them. Moving quickly to one side, they looked over their shoulders just as Sam's old pickup truck slowed down and stopped beside them.

"Want a lift?" Scott leaned over and opened the passenger door.

Before Allie could refuse, Trudy readily accepted, "Sure, thanks. The road's steeper than I had expected. I didn't know we were going to hike halfway up a mountain." Laughing, she waved Allie into the seat first. "After you."

A stubborn set to Trudy's full lips warned Allie not to make a scene about who was going to sit in the middle next to Scott. Allie sent her a veiled look, thinking, "I'll get even with you later," as she climbed into the truck beside Scott.

The truck was an old one, and Trudy's ample hips took up more than a third of the high, narrow seat. Allie did her best to keep from crowding Scott, but there was little she could do about the close quarters. As she sat beside him, she tried to ignore the effect of his body warmth, and the faint scent of spicy aftershave lotion that teased her nostrils. His hair was still moist from a recent shower, and she remembered how the dark strands had waved around his face when they'd gone swimming in a river pool. His profile was the same and yet different because his attractive masculine features were marred by unhappy lines in his forehead and around his mouth. He drove without looking at her, and she was uncomfortable in this forced intimacy.

Window lights were visible through the trees as he turned off the road and drove a short distance to a wide clearing in front of the house. Almost immediately the front door flew open, and Patrick's rangy frame filled the doorway.

Scott was aware of Allie's obvious relief as she got out of the car. When he'd offered a lift, he'd hoped that some of the earlier friction over the room painting might be set aside, but he'd felt her body stiffness as she tried to keep as much distance between them as the cab would allow. Undoubtedly the next two weeks would only increase the chasm that had already widened between them. Once the campers arrived, he planned to keep his distance from her and the others.

Accepting this dinner invitation had been spur of the moment. Even as he asked himself why on earth he'd let himself in for a whole evening with Allie, he knew the answer. He didn't want to be alone in the house with memories of his dad and Jimmy. The sooner he was finished with Rainbow Camp the better, he decided as he took a deep breath, put a smile on his face and followed Allie and Trudy into the house.

Dorie had dinner ready, and she shooed them into the kitchen with a flutter of her apron. They sat at a round table, and bowed their heads as Pat said his favorite grace. "Father, God, be our guest, and may this food to us be blessed."

The meal was beautifully simple and delicious: golden-brown stuffed pork chops, accompanied by fresh garden peas and a spinach salad. Rhubarb pie with wild strawberries was served with rich, amber coffee.

"It does my heart good to see you haven't lost your appetite," Dorie told Scott in a tone that suggested that there were other things about him that had been lost since she'd seen him last.

The O'Tooles were as hospitable as ever, but as the evening progressed, Scott realized that they were in the same place they'd been years ago when they first started working summers for his father. Contented with few luxuries, they still depended upon things they could grow, chickens and pigs they could raise and a goat they could milk. Patrick's handyman work brought in what little income they had during the winter months, and he wondered how they would replace the modest income that the two of them earned helping his father with the camp. If they weren't so shortsighted, they'd recognize that he was doing them a favor by selling off his dad's land. Any new development in the area would raise the value of everyone's property, and if the O'Tooles sold out at a huge profit, they could live more comfortably somewhere else.

Scott hadn't intended to put his thoughts into words, but there was a lull in the table conversation that invited a change in topic. The women had been talking about church affairs, and the new minister that both Trudy and Allie liked.

"Have you and Dorie thought about selling this place?" Scott asked Patrick as they were sipping their coffee and eating Dorie's delicious pie.

Both Patrick and Dorie lowered their forks almost as one, and looked at him as if he'd suddenly started speaking a foreign language. "Are you thinking of buying it?" Patrick asked dryly.

"No, of course not." Scott forced a laugh. He knew then that he should have kept his thoughts to himself.

"Land's sake, why would we be wanting to sell our home?" Dorie asked.

"Because you could get the kind of price that would put money in the bank."

"Money for what?" Dorie asked, frowning. "To buy another house? To live somewhere else not half as nice?"

Allie brushed her lips with a napkin to hide the smile on her face. Scott had stepped into the mud hole with both feet. Obviously, money was the wrong criteria to measure the O'Tooles' wealth of happiness. Didn't he realize that Pat and Dorie were living a life of peace, joy and contentment that a huge bank account could never replace? What saddened Allie was remembering that as a youth Scott had never talked about making big money as a goal in life, but the man sitting across the table from her had sadly settled on financial prosperity as the measure of his life. *What shall it profit a man if he gain the whole world, and lose his own soul?*

To ease the tension, Allie said, "What do you say we get the kitchen cleared, and then persuade Patrick to get out his guitar? Trudy and I have been harmonizing on some good old country tunes. We thought we'd do a couple for 'Skit Night' if Patrick would help us practice."

"I reckon I could strum a tune or two for a couple of pretty lasses," Patrick conceded as a smile creased his craggy face.

Scott suddenly felt out of place, and wished he'd stayed at the house. He had nothing in common with these people anymore. He couldn't see that they had matured at all.

As soon as he could, he got to his feet and he said,

"Thanks for the wonderful dinner, Dorie. I'm sorry but I'd better run along. I've got some business calls coming in later."

"Sure and you're always welcome at our table, Scott," Dorie said with a sincere smile. "I'm hoping we'll be seeing more of you while you're here. You'll probably be helping out with the young 'uns, won't you?"

"I'm afraid not," he answered quickly. "I really had planned to have everything wound up by now and get back to my brokerage business. Because of the delay, I've had to put a computer in one of the bedrooms so I can work from here. I don't expect to have any free time."

"'Tis a shame you can't take a little vacation for yourself," Dorie said sadly. "Especially since this is the last time that there'll be a Rainbow Camp."

"The property will be put to good use," Scott assured her. "There's no doubt that I'll get my price out of it."

"So you've made up your mind to sell out, have ya?" Patrick pushed back his chair and stood up.

"Yes, I have," Scott said firmly, looking the older man straight in the eyes.

"The Lord has made good use of that place for a good many years, and Sam was a good partner doing His work."

"There's a buyer all lined up to sign the papers," Scott said flatly. "It's a done deal."

"Maybe not," Patrick said. "Ever hear the saying, 'Man proposes, and God disposes'?"

Scott gave a short laugh. He wasn't going to argue.

He'd made his plans, and he'd learned the hard way not to trust anything or anyone, but himself.

"Oh, you can't leave now, Scott," Trudy protested. "That hike back to the camp will finish me off for sure. If you hadn't come along, I'd probably still be huffing and puffing to get here."

"If Scott wants to leave, I'll run you ladies back to camp," Patrick volunteered, giving Scott a dismissing wave of his hand. "Go on, son, tend to your business."

Allie surprised herself by jumping to Scott's defense. "Time has a way of running over us sometimes. Maybe it's a good idea if we all call it a night. Tomorrow is going to be another busy day."

Dorie nodded. "I got a hundred things to do in the kitchen, but we'll be ready for the children when they get here," she said with the air of a coach urging her team to victory.

After a few minutes of conversation about what preparations still had to be made, Allie and Trudy said good-night. They gave Dorie a hug as they prepared to leave and Scott thanked her for the wonderful meal.

"We'll take a rain check on the guitar playing," Allie reassured Patrick, knowing in her heart that there wasn't going to be any time for such idle happenings.

When Patrick saw the pickup parked out in front, he demanded, "Why are you driving Sam's old Ford when you got that fancy rental car?"

"I was thinking about leaving it with you. I thought you might know someone who could make use of it. I hate to junk it."

"Junk it!" He looked aghast. "You're out of your blithering mind. Why there's plenty of miles left in the old baby. Your dad and I spent many hours keeping it running. You'll not be junking it, if I have anything to say about it."

"Good," said Scott, silently smiling as he turned away.

Chapter Four

The church bus was ready and waiting to load at nine o'clock Monday morning. Allie and Trudy had come back to town for the weekend, and had pulled together all the loose ends for the group's stay at Rainbow Camp. Lily Twesbury and a middle-aged couple, Bob and Marie Tomlin, had all the supplies packed and ready to load on the bus.

As the youngsters began to arrive, Allie checked them off the list. "Stack your luggage over there so Barry can load it in the compartment."

"These kids are taking enough stuff for a month," Barry Nelson, the bus driver, complained. He shook his head as he surveyed the mountain stack of suitcases. A retired postman, he was the volunteer that drove the church bus whenever he was needed. He was a jovial fellow, claiming that after thirty years of "hoofing" it, he was always ready to take a ride. He wouldn't put up with any horseplay on the bus, and even the most rambunctious kids settled down when he was in charge. He did double duty as bus driver and chaperon on youth outings.

Allie had checked off all but two names on her list of youngsters when she realized that Randy hadn't showed up. *Oh, no,* she groaned inwardly. Was the belligerent boy going to be a no-show after all the work and effort she'd put into persuading him to come?

"What's the matter?" Trudy asked, seeing a flicker of exasperation on Allie's face.

"It's Randy. We're already fifteen minutes late leaving. I think he would have been here if he was going." She handed the list to Trudy. "Mary Ellen is the only other one who isn't here. Someone said she hurt her leg playing soccer on Saturday, so I doubt she'll be able to come. I'm going to run in and call Randy's foster parents and see what the story is."

When Allie asked if Randy had changed his mind about going to camp, Mrs. Sloan, his foster mother, was astounded. "Why Randy was up at the crack of dawn getting ready. Never have seen a kid so excited. Jim dropped him by the church an hour early. Are you sure he's not there?"

"He could be inside. Let me take a look around and call you back," Allie told her, thinking that maybe all the excitement had made the boy sick and he was in the restroom.

She stopped at the office first, but Harriet hadn't seen him. The church was built in an L-shape, with the sanctuary being the short leg of the building.

"Randy!" she called as she went through the church, and checked the restrooms. Allie's heart sank with disappointment. Maybe the boy had chickened-out and taken off before the bus got there. He could be blocks from the church by now.

She was about to give up when she poked her head into the last classroom, and there was Randy. He stood near one of the opened cupboards carrying a backpack that was so heavy it rounded his slender shoulders. When he saw her, he stiffened like a cornered animal ready to flee.

"Oh, there you are," Allie greeted him pleasantly, ignoring the guilty look on his face. *Caught in the act,* she thought. She knew there was nothing of great value in the Sunday school closets. What had he put in the backpack? Whatever it was, he must have really wanted it. She decided not to confront him with evidence of his obvious looting. First things, first. Getting the tough little boy on the bus and up to camp was the first order of business. "Come on, Randy, the bus is about ready to leave."

As she hurried him out of the church, he kept darting anxious looks at her, but she just chatted about the ride ahead. When she suggested that he let Barry put his backpack with the rest of the luggage, he stubbornly refused.

Trudy raised a questioning eyebrow as Allie turned around to Harriet who had come to see them off. "Will you call Mrs. Sloan and tell her that Randy's on the bus?"

"Sure thing. You guys have a wonderful time." She gave both Allie and Trudy a hug. "I'll say a prayer for you every day."

"Better say two," Allie said wryly as she saw Randy's belligerent face pressed against the window.

They finally got everyone settled in the bus, after much last-minute shifting around in seats. Excitement was almost thick enough to cut as the children laughed and chatted during the two-hour drive.

Allie sat in an aisle seat by Cathy so the quiet, shy little girl could look out the window. Her deep blue eyes were wide with wonder as the bus rolled along past grass-covered meadows, sunflower-lined roads and horse pastures where sleek mares stood by foals only a couple of months old.

Cathy's parents had been very nervous when they brought her to the bus. Obviously, this was the first time they'd entrusted their daughter's care to anyone outside the family.

"Cathy has special needs, you know," her mother had warned Allie as she handed her a list of things to watch for. "If she doesn't have her hearing aids turned on, she doesn't hear anything that's going on, and even with her hearing aids, she misses a lot. Cathy knows how to change the batteries, but sometimes she forgets."

"I'll be sure and check on them every morning," Allie had assured her. Allie impulsively gave Mrs. Crawford a hug and said softly, "Cathy's going to be fine. I'll take good care of her, I promise."

Allie felt a sudden wash of happiness as she looked down at the beaming eight-year-old who was taking in everything with a kind of wondrous awe. What joy to see the excitement on her face as her narrow world expanded beyond anything she had experienced before.

The O'Tooles were ready and waiting to greet the bus when it rumbled across the bridge and stopped in front of the main building.

Scott was nowhere to be seen, and Allie couldn't tell from the closed look about the house whether he was there or not. *It doesn't matter,* she told herself. He'd already warned them that he was going to be too busy to get involved in any of the camping activities. But that knowledge still didn't prevent her from hoping he'd show up anyway.

Scott was only vaguely aware of the invasion of the youthful campers during the day. He was ensconced in an upstairs bedroom, working on business matters, using his computer and the telephone. When daylight had faded, and the room was dark except for the radius of light from his desk lamp, he realized it was time to quit.

Weary and stiff from his sitting position, he went downstairs to scramble a couple of eggs and make toast for dinner. He was sitting at the kitchen table, listlessly eating his meal when the haunting beating of tom-tom drums reached his ears. He didn't need to look out the window to know what was happening.

For a moment it seemed that time had played a trick on him. In his mind's eye, he could see the leaping fire in the center of the camp where his dad had made an open stone fireplace. The spot was a favorite one for evening songs, stories and prayers. His heart tightened remembering how much Jimmy had liked to join in the evening sing-alongs, and the telling of ghost stories. Every night the two of them had lingered outside, looking up at the stars, reluctant to go to bed and making plans to sleep outside before the summer was over. They loved to pitch a tent near the river, and listen to its mesmerizing roar as the water tripped and fell over rocks in its rush down this side of the Continental Divide. They'd shared boyish secrets and dreams of adventures they would have when they reached manhood.

Scott put his head in his hands, wishing he were anywhere in the world but in this place of torment. He'd never considered himself a coward, but if running away from the past was a weakness, he was ready to give in to it. Why on earth had he allowed himself to be talked into delaying everything for two more weeks? His mother thought he was out of his mind, and he was beginning to believe it himself.

He allowed anger to cover up his loneliness as he strode around the house, sorting out things to be thrown away and making piles of pictures and books that the second-hand man might be interested in buying. Every closet and drawer assaulted him with memories; faint remembered scents teased his nostrils; everything in the house was a trigger to bring back feelings he wanted buried and forgotten.

For about an hour he heard the incessant drumbeats and waves of childish voices raised in Indian chants, and then the night took on an enveloping silence.

Good. He glanced at his watch. Eight-thirty. They'd be bedding the kids down for the night, and all would be quiet until six the next morning. He waited another fifteen minutes before wandering out on the porch. Ignoring the old swing, he leaned up against one of the porch posts and drew in a deep breath as he looked up at an evening sky that was like a velvet drape dotted with star spangles. He'd forgotten how pure and clean the air was at this altitude, away from the city's spoils. Beginning to feel relaxed, he sat down on the front steps where he had a good view of the center of the camp.

He instantly stiffened. "What?"

The campfire was still burning! Surely they hadn't forgotten to douse it thoroughly with water, but he couldn't see any dark figures anywhere near the radius of light.

All was quiet.

Muttering to himself, Scott picked up a bucket from the corner of the porch, hurried down the steps to the house and strode toward the blazing bonfire. Making sure that all of the fires were out had been one of the responsibilities that his father had given him every summer. Sam had lectured them all about unattended campfires.

When he reached the fire, he saw that a ring of rocks contained the blazing wood, but the wind was coming up and sparks were beginning to fly upward. There was always danger that some could be blown away from the open area and into the nearby trees and underbrush.

He strode angrily past the campfire, and headed toward the creek to fill his bucket. A winding path led through a wooded area before opening up to a grassy bank along the mountain stream's edge.

As Scott came out of the drift of trees, he stopped, startled to see a figure dipping water from the swift-flowing stream into a bucket. Moonlight touched Allie's blond hair like golden tinsel and as she stood up, Scott pulled back into the shadows.

That halcyon summer they'd spent as much time together as they could. Sharing all their camp chores was one of the ways they could be together, and dousing the campfire had been one of them. Nightly they had walked down to the stream together to get water. Even now, he remembered the soft feel of her hand in his, and the way she'd looked up at him as they walked together to and from the stream. They hadn't talked much. A soft laugh, a tender look and an amused smile were enough to convey an intimacy beyond words. That kind of closeness had been new to him that summer, and he'd never felt it with anyone else. Maybe some communion with another being belonged to the young and innocent.

As he watched her turn away from the river, and come up the path toward him, his courage failed. How could he meet her like this when all his senses were bombarding him with warring sensations? He quickly pulled back into a drift of thick pines, and blended into their shadows. The roar of the tumbling water had muffled his footsteps, and so she walked past him without knowing that he was only inches away.

He waited until she had put out the fire and had gone on the way to her cabin before he emerged from the trees. He strode back to the house and slammed the door shut behind him, as if he'd somehow escaped some nefarious entrapment from the past.

Chapter Five

On the nature walk the next day, the children taught Allie once again how to live joyfully in the moment.

"Look, Miss Allie, there's a blue jay!"

"Wow! That rock looks like a big elephant."

"Wild strawberries? Gee, can I eat one?"

The world was fresh and new in their eyes, and as Allie walked along with the bouncing children, she felt the slumbering child within her come to life again. How sad, she thought, that adulthood buried the wonderful traits of spontaneity, surprise and curiosity that were there in childhood. Seeing the fresh and exciting world through their eyes, Allie was filled with renewed wonder at God's magnificence. Jesus had taught that the way to enter the kingdom of heaven was to become childlike in trust, love and fullness of life. As they looked for flowers and birds and trees pictured in Lily's handout, Allie felt as if she were walking hand in hand with the child deep within herself.

Much to her delight and surprise Randy kept close to Cathy during these outings. He made sure that the little girl didn't miss anything, whether it was a red-breasted woodpecker in a tree, or a fragile yellow butterfly dancing over a blue field of wildflowers.

Cathy was the exception when it came to Randy showing his brash, tough side. The other children quickly learned not to invade his space. He was more than ready to shove someone else aside if they got in his way. Because of his aggressive behavior, he failed to endear himself to the adult supervisors. Allie was the only adult who could approach the hostile little boy without setting him off in an angry tirade.

"That one's a handful," Bob Tomlin told Allie. "I have to keep my eye constantly on him in the cabin. He shoves everyone around, takes what he wants, and I can't trust him a minute when my back is turned."

"I know," Allie agreed, sighing. "Randy's had to survive by his own wits for a long time. He's never known love or trust, and he's had to cope the best way he could. I'm not even sure he's in the best foster home for him. He's been constantly moved from one facility to another since the court took him away from his derelict mother. I'm just glad he'll have a chance to see a different side of life for a couple of weeks."

Bob looked skeptical. "It's going to take more than a couple of weeks to straighten that one out."

Allie decided not to mention Randy's stashed backpack to Bob. At the moment, she wasn't certain how to handle the theft. It might be a good idea to take a look at the loot before she did anything, she decided. Getting the boy in trouble wasn't going to improve the chances of him gaining some positive results from these two weeks at camp.

On one of the nature walks, Lily handed out tablets and pencils. "Now I want each of you to find a quiet place and sit very still until you've looked at everything around you. Then write about whatever you are seeing, hearing or touching," she told the group. "This is called journaling, and you don't have to show what you've written to anyone else if you don't want to. Just 'talk on paper' and don't worry about spelling or anything else."

Allie kept her eye on Randy as the children spread out. It would be just like him to disappear while he had the chance. She was relieved when he'd climbed a little way up the hillside and sat on a rock just a little distance from Cathy. She glanced up at him from time to time and saw that he wasn't making any effort to write. Obviously he didn't trust their teacher not to read anything he put down on paper and hold it against him. Trust was not something in his young life that had proven to be worth anything.

Cathy, in contrast, had her head bent over her paper as she wrote, and her mouth and eyes were scrunched up in earnest concentration. When she finished writing, she moved over to where Randy was sitting, and Allie saw their heads put together as Cathy read to him what she'd written. Randy smiled and nodded, obviously giving his approval.

Pleased that Cathy had shared her writings with Randy, Allie was still naturally curious and a little disappointed that she might never know what the two of them had shared. But her heart quickened when the little girl came over to where Allie was sitting and handed her the tablet. Cathy had written a poem.

If you were here,
You could touch the soft pine needles,
You could touch the cold, jagged rocks.
You could see beautiful summer flowers in bloom,
You could see colorful birds flying above in reds and blues.

If you were here,
You could taste the sweet wild berries,
You could taste the clear mountain water.
You could know the crackle of rocks beneath your feet,
You could know the trees blowing softly in the wind.
If you were here in the mountains.

Allie smiled her approval. "It's beautiful, Cathy."

"She can write good," Randy said with big-brother pride. He did, indeed, look and act like an older brother. He was big for his age—ten years old—and Cathy was small for her eight years. It warmed Allie's heart that they were a support for each other. Cathy needed someone to help her cope with her disability, and Randy needed someone to love. *Thank you, Lord,* Allie breathed when she saw how beautifully the two children gave to each other.

After the nature walk, and a picnic lunch by the stream, most of the children were ready to rest in their cabins during their free time. Trudy suggested to Allie that they pay Scott a visit while they had a little time to themselves.

"What on earth for?" Allie asked, instantly putting up her guard. Having another face-to-face confrontation with their reluctant benefactor was something she didn't need.

"I was thinking that there are probably a lot of things in the house that the church could make good use of for our next garage sale. It seems a shame to let him discard a bunch of stuff that could mean money for our youth projects, doesn't it? I mean, why not take advantage of his intentions to clear out the house and get rid of everything? I think it's our Christian duty to help him out, don't you think?"

Her expression was so innocent that Allie couldn't help but laugh aloud. Shaking her head, she said, "You are something else, Trudy Daniels. I don't know how you do it."

"Do what?"

"Use blackmail in such an innocent and angelic way. How can I say no when I'll have the youth projects on my conscience the next time we're trying to earn money?"

"I guess you can't," Trudy said smugly. "Come on. Let's clean up and then go face the lion in his den."

Scott had just hung up from a lengthy business call to one of his associates when he heard knocking on the front door. *What now?* he thought impatiently, glancing at his watch. Two o'clock? He couldn't believe he'd been at the computer all day, and missed lunch entirely.

He had a business dinner appointment scheduled that evening with some land speculators at a mountain restaurant about forty miles up the canyon. He'd been trying to get everything in order to close up the deal that night if possible. As he hurried down the stairs, his mind was filled with details yet to be taken care of before the evening meeting. The sooner he left Colorado the better.

When he opened the door and saw Allie and her friend standing there, he smothered instant irritation. He wasn't in the mood to deal with Allie Lindsey, nor the memories that had plagued him last night when she floated in and out of his restless dreams, sometimes laughing in that open free way of hers, and sometimes staring at him with clear-blue condemning eyes.

At the moment she wasn't doing either. She was politely distant, and the expression on her face was quite neutral. He had the impression that she wasn't any more pleased to see him than he was to see her.

Trudy was the only one smiling. "Well, here we are. Ready to look over your treasures, Scott. I hope this is an okay time for you. We've got all our little charges settled for a while."

"Oh, of course," he quickly recovered himself. "Come on in. I'm afraid everything is in a mess. I've been emptying out closets and drawers but haven't done anything with the stuff but pile it higher and higher."

"Maybe we could do a little straightening up for

you while we look over some of the discards." Trudy offered brightly. "I was telling Allie that we could use some donations for our youth garage sale. I mean, if you don't mind if we take a few things that we could resell."

"Not at all. Be my guest." He waved them in the house. "You could pile all the stuff you want in the front bedroom and arrange for someone to haul it into town before the house is leveled."

Leveled! Allie stared at him in disbelief. How could he talk in such a callous way about destroying the house that had been his father's home for so many years?

They followed him into the house, and as she stood in the center of the homey living room, she had an insight about Scott's seemingly callous attitude. His loneliness was almost that of a child crying in the dark—his outwardly indifferent behavior was his way of coping with a deep hurt and loss. She could almost hear Sam weeping for his son who had shut himself off from everyone, refusing to allow himself any emotion that might lighten the burden of his grief.

"Boy, you weren't kidding," Trudy said as she looked around at the congested room, every surface piled high with books, pictures, papers and mementos of a lifetime.

"And this is only one room," Scott said, threading his hair with his fingers. "If there'd been anything in the house worth anything I could have had one of those auction companies handle everything, but as you can see, no one would be interested in bidding on the contents. The only person who treasured this house and everything was my dad.''

Allie made a pretense of examining some stacked books to keep from looking at him. His voice betrayed the raw pain in his heart. She couldn't bear to see the emptiness in his eyes, and the stiffness of his lips. What could she say to help him heal his grief? Obviously, he was ready to reject any overture she might make, and seemed to even resist her very presence in the house. Tears threatened to spill from her eyes when he excused himself as soon as he could.

"I'll leave you both to your scavenger hunt," he said with a dismissing wave of his hand. "Just put everything that you want in the bedroom across the hall.''

"What about the furniture?" Trudy said with an acquiring eye.

Scott gave a short laugh. "Dad picked up all the furniture at a secondhand store. If you're looking for any antiques, you're out of luck. Sorry.''

"What about the piano?"

Allie put down a book and quickly looked at him. For a brief second she thought some emotion was going to break through that controlled exterior of his, but even as a shadow crossed his eyes, he shrugged. "Go ahead, take it if you think there's any music left in those battered keys.''

"What about Jimmy's guitar?" Allie asked gently, hoping for some sign of gentle remorse, but she was disappointed. His uncompromising armor was in place.

"I guess he's not going to be needing it, is he?

Aren't harps the choice of instrument in heaven?'' he asked with a sarcastic edge to his voice.

Trudy was quick on the uptake. "I'm holding out for a banjo myself. I know I'll never get the hang of one in this lifetime.''

Scott granted her a brief smile. "By all means, take the guitar. And anything else you see.''

He obviously wanted to avoid any further involvement in the picking and choosing of items for the church sale, and after he'd left the room and they heard him walking around upstairs, Trudy sighed. "Poor guy has a lot of healing to do, doesn't he?''

Allie nodded. "I was hoping that going through some of his father's things might make him realize that his dad led a full and happy life, even if he'd never accumulated much money.'' The house was filled with evidences of Sam's love of life, and the joy he had sharing it with others. Allie was saddened by Scott's determination to distance himself from anything that brought up the past even though there had been some treasured moments worth cherishing, moments that would have enriched his life at a time when he needed them the most.

"Well, I guess we'd better get started,'' Trudy said. "Let's take him at his word and fill that front bedroom with anything that might sell. This place looks like a garage sale waiting to happen.''

As they filled boxes with pictures, books and Western relics, they stacked them in a room, which obviously had been Sam's bedroom. His clothes still hung in the closet, and the dresser drawers were untouched.

Tears came to Allie's eyes as she opened a cigar

box sitting on the dresser, and saw a gold pocket watch that she remembered him showing to her that summer. She flipped open the lid to the bold black numbers and fragile hands of the watch. On the opposite side, a faded photo fit into the lid as if it were a locket. It was a picture of Scott and Jimmy when they were about eight and ten years old. Both boys wore broad grins and had tousled dark hair drifting down on their foreheads.

"Look at this." Allie showed the watch to Trudy. "I don't care what Scott says, I'm going to see to it that he doesn't give this away. Some day, he'll treasure it the way he should."

Trudy nodded. "Better not leave it in this room in case it gets mixed up with this other stuff."

Allie wanted to march upstairs and hand it to Scott. He'd disappeared with some vague muttering about getting ready for a business meeting that evening. Coward that she was, she put the box on the mantel beside a small pink polished rock that Sam must have brought up from the creek.

She glanced at her watch and saw with relief that free period was almost over. The sorting had taken more out of her than she would have believed. Maybe Scott had tried to do more about emptying the house than she'd given him credit for. No doubt he'd found it as draining as she had in spite of his hard-shell attitude.

Scott heard them leave and, after a few moments, he came downstairs to see how much progress they'd made. His father's bedroom was crowded with things they'd decided to take, and piles of discards littered the living room. As he looked around, he wished he could turn the key in the lock and never come back. The whole house was in a shambles.

His father's old cigar box sitting on the mantel caught his eye and almost without any conscious volition on his part, he took it down. His heart took a sickening plunge when he saw the watch inside. How well he remembered how his dad had lovingly taken the watch from his pocket every night and put it safely away in the faded box on the dresser.

Scott's fingers traced the smooth gold roundness of the watch but he didn't open it. He knew too well what lay inside. Blinking rapidly against an unbidden fullness spilling into the corners of his eyes, he quickly put the box back on the mantel, and turned away just as the telephone rang.

His voice was unduly husky when he said, "Hello."

"Scott?"

When his mother asked him if he was catching cold, he assured her, "I'm fine. I have a dinner appointment tonight with some investors interested in the property."

His mother launched into a five-minute lecture about holding firm in his negotiations. She warned him that land speculators were the worst when it came to buying low and then selling high. "You hold firm to the price we decided upon. It's about time your father's folly brought in some decent money."

Scott didn't want to go there. His mother had been vocal as long as he could remember about his father's lack of business sense so he said quickly. "I'm hoping that I may be able to get everything finalized before they serve dessert. If I do, it's possible I may be able to leave in a couple of days and take care of everything else from California."

'What about those church people?"

"The O'Tooles are handling everything. I don't need to be here."

His mother chided him again for complicating matters by letting them hold a youth camp when he was in the process of disposing of the property. "It was a foolish thing to do."

At the moment, he had to wholeheartedly agree with her. He certainly hadn't expected to be confronted with feelings that surfaced whenever he was around Allie. She challenged the protective shell he'd built around his heart and the sooner he put some distance between them the better.

Chapter Six

What was the matter now? When Scott appeared in the doorway of the dining room the next morning, Allie could tell from one quick look that he was a storm cloud about to break.

Her stomach muscles tightened. Rising quickly to her feet, she walked through the maze of tables filled with rambunctious children who were creating a joyful din that vibrated the rafters.

When she reached him, she offered a friendly, "Good morning" hoping the greeting might ease the scowl from his stony face. It didn't.

He motioned her out into the hall where they could hear themselves talk and said curtly, "I didn't know that you ladies were going to come back last night while I was gone. You might have told me. I would have left the door open so you didn't have to jimmy the old lock."

She looked at him blankly, not having the foggiest idea what he was talking about.

"It burns me that you upstanding church folk would violate a man's privacy so blatantly."

She couldn't believe what he was saying. "Are you accusing us of breaking into your house while you were gone?"

Drawing an impatient breath, he said, "When I got home, I found the house in even greater shambles than before. Not that I care about the stuff. I told you that I'm going to have it all carried off one way or another. By the end of next week, this whole camp will be fodder for a bulldozer, anyway. It's just that—"

"You think we took advantage of you," she finished sharply. "You think that Trudy and I sneaked into your house while you were gone and took more stuff that you'd already given us. Is that it?"

"That's what it looks like to me."

"For heaven's sake, Scott, what has happened to your common sense? Trudy and I were not in your house last night."

"Then who?"

"I don't know, but I'm sure that there's a reasonable explanation."

"Well, when you think of one, let me know. I'd like to have my dad's watch back."

"Oh, Scott, I'm sorry." Impulsively she touched his arm, and then quickly dropped her hand when she felt the rigid tension of his muscles.

Scott's forehead furrowed for a moment. "A couple of fellows came by late in the day to look at a compresser Dad had in the garage. They decided it was too old and left without buying it." He'd completely forgotten about them. He looked thoughtful and a little sheepish. "They did ask about the house furnishings, but I told them I'd already arranged to dispose of them."

"Do you think they came back after dark and went through the house?"

"That's a possibility," he admitted. "But why not take the computer? It's the only new thing in the house. A thief wouldn't take an old watch and ignore a two-thousand-dollar computer setup."

"Not a smart one," Allie agreed. "But rest assured, Trudy and I weren't anywhere near your house last night."

An embarrassed warmth crept up into his face. "I guess I was a little too hasty in jumping to conclusions. I'm sorry, Allie. Things aren't moving as fast as I would like. I had a disappointing meeting with some investors last night. They are suddenly dragging their feet. It's obvious they want the land for practically nothing so they can jack up the price and fleece builders who want to put up condos in this area." His mouth tightened in a firm line. "They don't know I'm used to dealing with the big boys. I can hold my own when it comes to negotiating a business deal as they're about to find out." Then his voice softened. "I'm wound up a little tight."

"What you need is a nice brisk hike up to Crescent Lake," she said impulsively. That had been a special place for them that summer. Did he remember the warm ledge of rocks leaning out over the water, and the way they had sat there reading their meditation verses and talking about a divine purpose to their lives? "Why don't you join us this afternoon?"

"Can't," he said shortly. "I've got another buyer coming by who seems ready to close the deal. I need to get some legalities taken care of so I can be ready to draw up the papers. Dad wasn't very good about taking care of recording deeds and the such, but once I get a signed contract, I can get everything cleared away in a couple of days."

"Then you'll be leaving?"

He nodded. "Nothing to keep me here once the papers are signed."

"No, I suppose not. To be perfectly honest, Scott, I was hoping that we might find our way back to the friendship that we once had," she said sadly. The shadow of regret was in her lovely eyes and voice now as she looked at him. "I guess it was just wishful thinking on my part that some of the feelings we had for each other still remained somewhere deep within each of us."

Scott was startled when her regretful tone swept him back to the day that summer camp had ended and they'd kissed goodbye. Even as they had promised not to let college life put any distance between them, it was as if they both knew even then that the tide of life would sweep them in different directions. The enchanting young love that had been between them had slowly faded away, and neither had made a real effort to keep it alive.

The moment of remembrance was almost too much for him. Why was she bringing up all of this now? He wasn't the naive, wide-eyed innocent that he had been then. Harsh reality had taught him lessons that she wouldn't begin to understand. He covered up a sudden rush of emotion by firming his chin, and saying, "It's been great seeing you again, Allie. Really it has. I wish all the best for you and maybe our paths will cross again sometime." He heard himself saying, "If you ever get to Long Beach, give me a call."

For a moment she didn't answer, and then her voice was as devoid of emotion as his. "I'll do that," she said with a false smile. She knew he would be around for a few more days, but he acted as if he were anxious to say goodbye.

He turned and left the dining room, and she went back to her table. When breakfast was over, the children filed into the activities room for "Sharing Time."

Lily had decided that every morning an adult would collect five or six children in a circle, and encourage them to share anything they wanted with the small group. They could talk about anything they liked, tell a story or bring something for "show and tell."

Allie had five little girls in her group, and one of them was Cathy. Because of her hearing difficulty, she wasn't as vocal as the other girls, but Allie made sure that she was included by often slowly repeating what had been said so Cathy could lip-read.

After all the other girls had taken their turn, Cathy tugged on Allie's sleeve. Her freckled face wore a huge smile and her eyes danced with excitement.

"Yes, Cathy, it's your turn. What do you want to share?" Allie was delighted to see the eagerness on the little girl's face. Until then, Cathy had been very reluctant to offer anything to the group.

Cathy reached into her sweater pocket for something, and then held out her hand. Slowly she opened her fingers to show a beautifully polished pink rock.

Allie stared at the stone. She couldn't believe it. A fuzzy and indistinct memory began to form in her mind's eye. She'd seen it before. Yes, it was the same rock. She was positive. The pink stone was the one that had been lying on the fireplace mantel next to the cigar box in Scott's house.

"Isn't it pretty?" Cathy asked shyly, searching Allie's face.

"Lovely," Allie murmured, turning it over in her hand. Discouraging Cathy when she'd made an overture to share with the group was the last thing Allie wanted. She certainly didn't want the little girl to pick up any negative vibes around her offering. "It's a beautiful color."

"Pink, like cherry blossoms," Cathy said, her poet heart coming to the front.

"Or a pink candy," one of the other girls offered.

As Cathy passed the stone around for everyone to admire, Allie struggled to collect her thoughts.

"Ooooh, it's so smooth," another girl murmured as she stroked the stone. "Where'd you find it, Cathy?"

Cathy just smiled and didn't answer. This was the little girl's usual demeanor either when she didn't hear, or when she didn't want to try and answer a question. The other girls were used to Cathy's silence, so they didn't press her as they would have anyone else in the group.

In any other circumstances, Allie would have let it pass, but as soon as the group broke up, she turned to Cathy. Positioning herself so the girl could easily read her lips, Allie smiled and said slowly, "I love your pretty rock. Did someone give it to you?"

Eyes shining, Cathy nodded.

"A good friend?"

Cathy nodded again. Then with a shy smile, she said, "Randy."

Allie's stomach took a sickening plunge. Without a doubt, Randy was Scott's thief. She remembered then that Bob Tomlin had said that he caught Randy trying to sneak out at night. Apparently, the boy had been successful the night before. The gift he'd given Cathy was evidence that he was guilty of breaking into Scott's house.

What to do? For Randy's sake, she didn't want the truth to get out. All her hopes of changing his behavior would be lost if he was branded a thief. He would just try to live up to their expectations. *I have to handle this myself.*

She waited for a chance to talk to him, and while the others were getting organized into teams for volleyball, she managed to get him aside. "Let's take a walk, Randy. I need to talk with you."

"Why?"

"I think you have something to show me." She could almost see the hairs instantly bristle on his head.

"No, I don't." A pugnacious scowl crossed his face. "I want to play volleyball."

"Later." Her voice was even, but firm as she led the way to his cabin.

She motioned him inside, then walked over and sat down on the bunk that she knew was his. She was pretty sure the things he'd taken from the church were still in his backpack. She didn't want him to know that Cathy had given him away by showing the rock, so she decided to tackle the church theft first.

"What do you have in your backpack, Randy?"

"Nothing."

"Nothing?" She peered under the bunk. "Looks like it's pretty full to me. What's in it?"

She could almost see his mind working. How much did Allie know? What lies would serve him best? Could he lie his way out of this?

"I know you took some things from the church cupboard the day we left," Allie said firmly. "What did you take, Randy?"

A hard lump moved in his throat and then with a defiant glare, he said, "Books."

She stared at him as she tried to cover her astonishment. Books were the last thing in the world she would have thought interested Randy enough to steal. His school teachers reported that they had coaxed, threatened and pleaded for him to hit the books, but he refused. Even though the boy could read well enough, he chose not to spend any time doing it.

"Why, Randy?" she asked in what she hoped was a normal voice.

He glared at her. "Cathy's parents didn't want her

reading all the time. She was worried. She said she could only bring a couple of books. I told her not to worry. I'd find some for her.''

''So you took the books for Cathy?''

''There was a bunch of books in those cupboards, all kinds. At night, when all the other girls are talking, she needs something to do,'' he said in a lecturing tone that made Allie silently smile. ''Don't you be blaming her. I was the one who took them.''

''So you gave Cathy all the books?''

He nodded.

''If you gave all the books you had in your backpack to Cathy, why does it still look full?''

''It's not full, it's empty,'' he lied with childish defiance.

She reached under the bunk and pulled out the bulging backpack. ''Randy, I don't want to see what's inside now,'' she said as she handed it to him. ''But I want you to bring it along. We're going to pay a visit to someone.''

On the way to Scott's house, she prayed for guidance. On some intuitive level, she felt that Randy should be the one to put the stolen watch in Scott's hands. The boy trudged beside her like a captive being led to the gallows.

When they reached the front door, it was obvious that the old lock had been broken, and she glanced down at Randy with a questioning raise of her eyebrows.

The look he gave her was both guilty and edged with a hint of pride as if she ought to be admiring his handiwork. She half-expected him to remark on the job he'd done getting into the house.

"Randy, my boy, you're something else," she said in an affectionate tone.

The door opened before they knocked, and Allie knew that Scott must have been sitting on one of the couches in front of the window. His glance went from her to the boy and back again.

"Well, hello," he greeted them in a questioning tone. "What's happening?"

Allie said quickly. "Scott, this is Randy Cleaver. He's come to have a talk with you, and it's important that you take a few minutes to hear what he has to say." Her eyes warned him that she wasn't going to accept any excuses that he was too busy.

"All right," he said reluctantly. Didn't she know that his youth counseling days were long over? What in the blazes was going on?

"I think it would be better if I waited here on the porch. What Randy has to say would be better man-to-man."

Scott looked completely baffled, and Randy looked ready to bolt. She prayed that she was doing the right thing.

"It's all right." She gave the boy's shoulder a re-assuring squeeze. "Scott was young once. In fact, he may have a story or two to share with you, once you tell yours. I'm sure he hasn't forgotten his old friend, Benny Wade."

She gave Scott a smile that was more a warning than anything. "I'll sit here on the porch while you have your little chat."

She turned and walked away from the door.

Scott had little choice but to take the boy inside. *What's going on here?* Scott couldn't imagine why Allie had brought Randy to the house for a "chat." The kid looked like a cornered rabbit ready to bolt.

"All right, Randy. What's this all about?" Scott asked as kindly as he could as they stood in the middle of the living room.

Randy wiggled out of the backpack and dropped it on the floor. "There." He gave the backpack a kick in Scott's direction, and waited to see what Scott was going to say or do. "Take it. I don't want your dumb stuff." His body was poised, stiff and ready for any physical abuse that might come his way.

Your dumb stuff. The light went on in Scott's head. *Oh, so that's it.* The frightened boy glaring at him was the one who had broken into the house. He could tell the kid was prepared for physical punishment, so Scott acted only slightly interested in the whole matter. "You're bringing back all the things you took?" Scott said evenly as if he'd known all along who the thief had been.

Randy clamped his mouth shut as if he wasn't going to incriminate himself by saying anything more.

Scott picked up the backpack and loosened the straps. There on top was the old cigar box. Scott quickly opened it, and saw with a spurt of relief that his dad's watch was still nestled inside. The other things in the bag were inconsequential, but the theft of his father's watch had aroused unexpected feelings in Scott, and made him admit emotions that he'd been trying to bury.

"Do you make a habit of breaking into other people's houses?" Scott asked in a conversational tone as he put the cigar box back on the mantel. He knew turning his back on the boy was an invitation for the kid to bolt, but when he turned around Randy was still standing stiffly in the middle of the floor, waiting for his punishment.

In a weird moment of déjà vu Scott remembered standing almost in the same spot in this very room when his father asked him and Jimmy a similar question. "Why would you break into someone else's home?"

Scott's thoughts sped back to the summer he and Jimmy had made friends with Benny Wade, a tough little guy who quickly made life interesting by leading them into a series of escapades. The most serious was breaking into a vacant summer cottage. Scott lifted a portable radio and was caught when he and Jimmy tried to sneak it into their bedroom. Now he knew why Allie had brought up Benny.

"It's all there," Randy was saying with the aggressive stance of a liar.

"All of it?" Scott prodded. Getting the watch back was all he cared about, but he was intrigued by the boy's insistence that nothing was missing. "I don't think so. What have you held back, Randy?"

He worked his lips, and then dropped his gaze to the floor. "The pink rock."

Scott only vaguely remembered the polished stone that had been on the mantel. "You kept the pink rock?"

Randy's head came up and his eyes blazed. "I gave it to Cathy, and you can't have it back."

"I see," Scott said, intrigued by this tough little boy's attitude about something he'd given a girl. "You gave the rock away?"

He jutted out his little chin in a pugnacious way. "Cathy likes things like that 'cause she got things in her ears that don't help her hear much. She likes things like rocks and flowers."

"Well, I think you're right. She should keep the rock. Now, about that little talk." Scott could almost feel his dad looking over his shoulder. "What do you say we take a couple of fishing poles down to the creek and spend a little time thinking about this?"

Scott remembered how bewildered he and Jimmy had been when their dad had suggested the same thing. He also remembered the lesson he'd been given that day. As the three of them had sat on the bank waiting for a fish to bite, his father had ordered them to take deep breaths of the pine-scented air. "You boys forgot that God made enough air for everybody. And enough sunshine for every living thing. You dishonor Him when you think that you have to take from someone else because there's not enough of God's goodness for you. I want you to think about that."

The radio was returned and the incident was never mentioned again. Scott had never heard of Benny Wade after that summer, but looking at Randy reminded him of the lonely little boy who had been trying to fill his life with other people's things.

"What do you say? Would you like me to show you how to catch a nice pink trout? I know a deep hole where they love to hide. I bet we can do a little talking and fishing. What do you say?''

Randy looked completely bewildered. Was this punishment? Going fishing? His expression eased into a big smile as he nodded.

A few minutes later, when Scott and Randy came out of the house, carrying fishing poles, Allie thought she must be hallucinating. Randy had a weathered fishing basket hung over his shoulder, and Scott was carrying a tackle box. Even though she'd been trying to keep her thoughts positive about what was going on inside the house, she wasn't in the least prepared for the air of reconciliation radiating between the two.

''I'm going to borrow Randy for the afternoon. We're going down to the creek.'' He winked at her. ''Fishing always clears a man's thinking, you know.''

She wanted to hug him for handling Randy in such a beautiful way. At that moment, she couldn't believe how much Scott looked like the personable young man who had been such a good youth counselor when she knew him. As she watched the man and boy head down the path toward the stream, walking side by side in rhythmic stride, her eyes were suddenly moist and her heart was full.

God certainly moved in mysterious ways, his wonders to perform.

Chapter Seven

When Allie told Trudy what had happened between Scott and Randy, she got a twinkle in her eye. "So our good-looking Scrooge may have a crack in that tough armor of his after all. I wouldn't have expected him to show any real concern about the missing watch, not after the way he dismissed the piano and the guitar."

"I know. No one was more surprised than I was when he lit into me because he thought we'd taken it."

"Well, if he'd accused me of breaking into his house, fireworks would have gone off all over the place," Trudy vowed. "The very idea makes me want to knock some sense into that handsome head of his."

"When I took Randy to see him, I didn't know what to expect," Allie admitted. "I guess I was just hoping that not all his affinity for young kids had been lost in his corporate world."

Whatever had gone on between him and Scott,

Randy wasn't saying. Allie learned from Cathy that Randy had caught three fish that afternoon, but that was all. Allie was relieved that the incident had been settled without anyone else in the camp the wiser.

"Trudy, you should have seen how skillfully Scott handled tough kids like Randy when they got out of line. He wasn't a pushover, by any means, but they learned to respect him. I know that if Randy could be around him even a little bit, we'd see some good things happening."

"Well, unless he starts spending time with the kid in the next few days, there isn't much chance that the two of them are going to develop any kind of a friendship."

"I can always hope," Allie said stubbornly.

The days were busy ones at the church camp, filled with outdoor activities, Bible studies, handicraft projects and evening programs. All of the chaperons had their hands full trying to guide a bunch of rambunctious youngsters who were like colts bounding in every different direction. Some of the children wanted to recite poems or sing songs, and others decided to write their own skits. As it turned out, Allie's hope that Scott might be drawn into the camp activities because of Randy never materialized.

Patrick told Allie that Scott was spending time in Denver taking care of business, and the only way Allie knew that he had returned was a trail of smoke coming out of the house chimney several evenings later.

"Yeah, he's back," Patrick said when Allie asked

him about Scott. "I reckon everything's a done deal except signing a few papers." He shook his head. "Good old Sam must be turning in his grave. A sad thing it is. He had high hopes for them boys of his, Sam did. Told me once that he was hoping Scott or Jimmy might come back and take over Rainbow Camp when the time came. Now one of them is gone, and the other can't get rid of this place fast enough."

"What went wrong, Patrick?" Allie asked sadly.

"Life," he answered in one word.

Surprised at the simple answer, she echoed, "Life?"

He nodded. "Life happens to everyone, Allie. Some folks hold steady to the rudder of faith when the storms hit, and others turn loose and get washed overboard into a sea of resentment and disbelief. That's what's happening to Scott. He has lost his hold on the strong faith his dad had given him. Now, he's adrift. Some people live their whole life that way. Let's pray to the good Lord that Scott isn't one of them."

When a weather report warned them to expect rain the next couple of days, Lily decided to move up "Skit Night" in the schedule. In place of the usual outdoor activities, the children in each cabin would stay indoors during the rainy afternoon and work up some kind of act for a program that evening.

Allie was a floating counselor, so she popped in and out of the cabins, helping with ideas, costumes and other theatrical props. The boys in Bob Tomlin's cabin decided to dress up as strong men of the Bible and act out one of the Biblical stories.

"What do you think, Allie?" Bob asked when she offered to help.

"Sounds like a good idea to me," she reassured him, but she was a little concerned when Randy chose to be young David with a slingshot, killing the giant, Goliath. The slingshot that he managed to make out of wood and rubber bands was big enough to hurl a river pebble quite a distance. The way Randy was handling it made her nervous.

"Why don't we make a target?" she suggested as innocently as she could, reasoning that if they placed the target against the back wall of the activity room and he missed, he wouldn't hit anything but wood. "You could draw a picture of the giant as a target and show everyone what a good shot you are."

His eyes sparkled. "I draw a mean warrior," he admitted with childish bragging. "I bet I can hit that bugger right between the eyes."

"Good. Let's see if we can find some poster board and some paints." She just hoped someone didn't set off Randy's temper while he was in the role of the great giant slayer with the slingshot ready for action.

"What are you and I going to do?" Trudy asked Allie, when she cornered her, trying to put together some costumes for the girls in that cabin.

Allie groaned. She'd forgotten that the adults were expected to participate. "I haven't the foggiest."

"How about us harmonizing on a couple of songs? We could run up to the house and get Jimmy's guitar.

If you still remember a few chords, we could work something up.''

Allie wanted to protest that she wasn't up to playing for an audience, even one as benign as the camp kids. She strummed now and then on her guitar, but strictly for her own pleasure. Trudy had a nice alto voice that harmonized with her light soprano and they had shared some fun at church sing-alongs.

''Do you have a better idea?'' Trudy asked with her usual bluntness. ''All right then. Let's get the guitar. It should still be in the bedroom with the rest of the things—unless our friend decided to give it to someone else. Do you want to run up to the house, or shall I?''

''You go,'' Allie said readily. No telling how Scott would react. Asking Scott for Jimmy's guitar was not high on her list of things to do. Trudy could carry it off better than she could. ''But don't insist,'' she warned. ''If he's changed his mind about giving it away, let it be.''

Trudy looked at her, puzzled. ''What makes you think he's changed his mind?''

''I'm not sure he knows what he wants these days,'' she said flatly.

Scott was in the kitchen, deciding to fix an omelette for supper when he heard a pounding on the front door and someone yelling, ''Open up. It's raining out here!''

Shoving the carton of eggs back into the fridge, he hurried down the hall. ''Come in,'' he yelled before he reached the door.

It flew open and Trudy dashed in as water streamed off her red plastic cape and matching umbrella. Her short black hair clung in damp strands around her wet face.

"Have you got a boat to let?" she asked with a hearty laugh. "We could use one if this keeps up. Brr. What kind of weather is this for June?"

"Haven't you heard? When it's springtime in the Rockies, it's the fourth of July every place else?" He smiled. "Come on over by the fire. You look like a wet poodle with your hair soaked like that."

"Thanks a lot. Just what a woman wants to hear."

Scott was a little uneasy. He couldn't imagine why Trudy had weathered the rain to pay him a visit. Had Allie sent her? Was something wrong? The possibility that Allie was in trouble brought an unexpected tightening in his chest. She had been on his mind all the drive to Denver and back. The business with Randy showed that her soft, compassionate nature hadn't changed a bit. She'd always been willing to stick her neck out for the underdog even when she was the one who ended up holding the bag.

"Are you a messenger who never lets the weather detain you from your appointed rounds?" he asked as subtly as he could, trying to find out quickly what her business might be.

"Not a messenger, exactly. I'm here on a mission."

"Oh, and what mission is that?" He felt himself relaxing a bit. Nothing about her manner signaled any crisis.

"Well, tonight is 'Skit Night.' You remember those

wonderful, horrible performances, don't you? Everybody gets in the act. Allie and I have done a little singing together at church, and we thought we'd try harmonizing on a couple of tunes while she strummed a few chords on the guitar. Jimmy's guitar, that is, if you don't mind us making use of it for tonight.''

"Of course not. I told you to take it. Why did you leave it here?" He was truly annoyed that the subject had come up again.

"We just wanted to make sure that—"

"Don't make such a big production out of it," he cut her off. "Take it."

"Sorry," Trudy said quickly, determined not to let his curtness make her lose her own temper. "We put the guitar with the other things in the bedroom. I'll just get it and be on my way."

"You should have taken it with you earlier," he said. "Saved you a trip out in this rain."

"I'm not fragile,' she said as she brushed by him. She went across the hall to the bedroom, and came out with the guitar. "I'll hide it under my cape to keep the case dry. Thanks again."

He tried to lighten the moment as he walked to the door with her. "Good luck. Break a leg and all that. Tell Allie I know she'll do herself proud."

She looked him squarely in the eyes. "Why don't you come down from that high-and-mighty tower of yours and tell her yourself?"

His mouth dropped open as a sharp reply formed on his lips, but Trudy didn't wait to hear it. She went out the door and disappeared in a curtain of gray rain.

* * *

"That man," she fumed to Allie a few minutes later when she stomped into their cabin and tossed the guitar case down on the bed. "Would you believe it? He chewed me out for not taking the guitar when he said we could have it. What gives with him, anyway?"

Allie's expression was pensive. "I don't think he really wanted to give Jimmy's guitar away."

"Then why is he in such a hurry for us to get it out of the house?"

"Because he's in denial. Sometimes that happens when someone loses a loved one. Scott might have been able to accept his dad's passing, but coming on top of Jimmy's tragic death, he's lost faith in himself and God. I'm afraid he's locked up his grief and heartache and he's trying to throw away the key." Her voice caught and she swallowed hard to keep back a surge of emotion that threatened to bring tears to her eyes.

Trudy sat down on the bed, and put her arms around Allie. "Honey, there's nothing you can do about it. You can't fight his battles for him."

"I know, but if you could have only known him, Trudy." Her voice grew husky. "He was so outgoing, so giving and full of enthusiasm. That summer was one of the happiest in my life. We used to walk up to the lake, sit on a rock, read poetry or just drink in all the beauty around us." She smiled wistfully. "Everyone loved being around him."

"With all that charm, I'm surprised he never married," Trudy said with a little gravel in her tone. "But then, maybe you just saw him at his best. Anyway, you've got to quit tearing your self up over the guy." She gave Allie's shoulders a squeeze. "Come on, we've got to do a little practicing if we're going to wow 'em tonight."

By seven o'clock the campers had finished eating dinner and were settled in the adjoining activity hall, waiting for the show to begin. Allie was in charge of getting the performers on and off the stage in the order of their appearance. The room fairly rocked with excitement. Lily Twesbury had brought a supply of costumes from the church's collection, and some of the children had been creative in making their own.

No first night performance was received with more enthusiasm than a group of angels who sang and floated around the small stage. A band of chanting Indians followed the angels and the floorboards bounced with their rhythmic dance steps. Patrick and Dorie O'Toole did an Irish jig that had everybody clapping in lively rhythm.

Allie was concentrating so hard on keeping things moving that she was startled when Trudy came up behind her and whispered, "He's here."

She didn't have the foggiest notion of what Trudy was talking about.

"Scott. He's here. Sitting in the back."

"Really?" Allie stilled an impulse to turn her head and look. "Thanks for telling me. Now I really feel much better about playing and singing," Allie said sarcastically.

"I dared him to come," Trudy said smugly.

"Then I'll deal with you later," Allie promised, and turned her attention back to the next skit.

When it was Randy's turn to mount the stage as David, Killer of Giants, Allie breathed a silent prayer that everything would go well. The boy had followed her suggestion and made a large poster with a figure of a giant as a target. Purposefully he walked to the middle of the stage. Then as he stood with his back to the audience, he drew a stone from a bag hanging on the belt of trousers that had been made one Christmas for a shepherd in a nativity scene.

Slowly and deliberately with a showmanship flair, he put the stone in his slingshot. Then he took aim, slowly pulled back on the rubber band, held it for a long moment of anticipation and then let it go. The stone struck the poster, and tore through the giant's head.

The audience clapped and yelled and Allie let out the breath she'd been holding. Randy turned around, swelled up like he had just won an Olympic medal.

Then the unbelievable happened!

Instead of walking off the stage, Randy took another pebble out of his bag, and loaded it in his slingshot.

"Randy, no!"

Allie's voice was lost in the clamor of the cheers and yells. Before she could bound out on the stage and stop him, he took aim at a light hanging over a doorway at the far end of the room. With unbelievable accuracy, the stone sailed across the heads of the audience, and shattered the bulb into a thousand fragments.

Luckily no one was standing in the doorway.

Scott automatically ducked but none of the fragments reached the back row of seats. What a shot! He was amazed that Randy had actually hit the light at that distance. When he saw Allie rush out and hurry Randy off the stage, he smothered a smile. Allie had her work cut out for her with that boy. From the way she'd handled the break-in, he knew that she was fond of the kid. But from just the little bit of time he'd spent talking to Randy while they were fishing, Scott knew the boy needed a firm, strong hand if he was going to overcome drunken parents and a series of foster homes.

Scott left his seat long enough to get a lightbulb from a utility closet where his dad had kept them. He quickly replaced the bulb with murmured thanks from the other adults, and then sat down again.

After Randy's dramatic performance, Scott was tempted to leave but Trudy's challenge kept him in his seat. Her biting remark about his being high-and-mighty had found its mark. He didn't care what Trudy thought about him, but Allie's opinion was another matter.

He rather enjoyed the variety of songs, dances and skits but he was impatient for Allie and Trudy's number. When it was their turn, he watched Allie walk out on the stage with the same easy grace he remembered. She wore a simple yellow summer dress that flowed from her narrow waist and swung gently around her shapely legs. Even though her figure had matured, she still retained the natural feminine youthfulness of the young girl who had captured his heart that summer.

Trudy took a place beside Allie at the microphone. Dressed in overalls, with a farmer's straw hat stuck on the back of her round head, she quipped with the audience and even took time for a "knock, knock" joke which the kids loved. Trudy was a ham, all right, Scott thought, but it was Allie he'd come to see.

With Jimmy's guitar slung over her shoulder, she lowered her head slightly as her fingers found the chords, and Scott's heart caught as they began singing their first song. Her hair looked soft and golden as it drifted forward on her cheeks, and as her sweet voice blended with Trudy's, he knew that coming had been a mistake. His chest was suddenly tight. Moisture beaded on his hands. A deep longing that he had thought forever stilled reached out and touched his deepest self.

When she looked across the audience to where he sat, he argued with himself that what he'd felt for her had been an innocent and adolescent love. In a few days she would be out of his life again, and he knew that she would never give her heart to anyone who did not have the same strong spiritual convictions as she did. There was no way to go back to that adolescent optimism they'd shared that summer. That was then; this was now.

As an overhead light caught the decorative trim on Jimmy's guitar, he remembered the day his dad had given it to his brother. Jimmy had been beside himself, and all that summer, he'd spent hours playing until his fingertips were raw. Unbidden memories poured through Scott's mind with bittersweet pain until suddenly, he came out of his reverie with a jerk.

He couldn't believe it! Allie and Trudy were singing, "Puff, the Magic Dragon." They had chosen Jimmy's favorite song, the one he had played over and over again the last summer they were here. Scott and Allie had sat together, holding hands, laughing and singing the lyrics as Jimmy strummed the chords on his guitar.

How could she?

Without waiting until the song was over, he left the building. Bending his head against the onslaught of wind and rain, he sloshed through mud and water back to the house. Flashes of lightning in the sky and cannonlike thunder matched the tumult raging within him. He couldn't wait to get away from this place. Only two more days and the papers would be signed. Then he could leave, and do everything else from his California office.

As he slammed the door behind him, and stomped through the silent house, he was angry with Allie for choosing to play Jimmy's song, and angry with himself for caring one way or the other.

"I was a fool to even go," he said to the empty kitchen, and then went upstairs to his computer, determined to lose himself in work.

Since Jimmy's death, the demands of his brokerage business had been a lifesaver. When something triggered the deep sorrow he was trying to forget, he could retreat to reports, demands and daily financial crises.

But not tonight. After a fruitless hour of trying to

make himself concentrate, he gave up. The storm outside didn't help his restlessness. Wind gusts made an eerie whistling under the eaves, and the old house moaned and creaked from the onslaught of driving rain.

He'd just fallen asleep when, shortly after midnight, he was jerked awake. At first, he didn't know what had awakened him. Then he realized there was a loud banging on his door, accompanied by the shrill siren of a police car.

Chapter Eight

"Flood waters coming. Evacuate now!"

For a bewildering moment, Scott struggled to take in the impact of the policeman's words.

"Do you hear me? Move!" the policeman ordered impatiently. "We've got to get everyone out of here—now. The whole canyon's flooded and a wall of water is coming down the river from above."

A surge of adrenaline shot through Scott. He knew what happened when flash floods in the mountains rushed down to the valleys below. Entire mountain communities were flooded, buildings were destroyed and summer homes and cabins lying along the river were washed away. He couldn't believe this was happening. It had been a hundred years since this canyon had experienced any kind of a life-threatening flood. He fought back a surge of panic. "How much time do we have?"

"Maybe a half hour, if we're lucky. I stopped at

Patrick's place first. He said you've got a whole camp full of kids.''

Scott's chest tightened as he remembered the crowded activity room only a few hours earlier. ''The cabins are full. Twenty-five to thirty people.''

''Start getting them loaded on the bus. I've got to get on downstream and warn as many people as I can. The river bridges are likely to go out any time. Get everybody out of here as fast as you can. Understand?''

''Yes, sir.''

The policeman turned away, stomped down the porch steps, and the small circle of his flashlight was lost in the swirling curtains of rain.

Scott thew on his clothes, scrambled in the kitchen drawers until he found a flashlight of his own, and then bounded out of the house. As soon as he had everyone on the bus, he'd come back and rescue important papers and disks from his desk.

The camp was still in darkness except for a few outside lights. Apparently the fury of the storm had drowned out the policeman's siren and the warning had not reached any of the cabins. How was he going to warn everyone in time?

As he stepped off the porch, he realized that they had completely misjudged the storm's fury. He was nearly lifted from his feet as the inferno of windblasts and lashing rain engulfed him. The rising river's deafening roar sounded like that of an animal rumbling in pain.

In flashes of lightning, he could see that rushing waters were already sweeping over the river's bank.

Like a greedy tongue, floodwaters were sucking and pulling vegetation into the thickening mass of mud, water and debris. As he put his head down and plunged forward at a run toward the first cabin, he heard someone calling.

"Scott! Scott!"

His name was barely audible in the stormy on-slaught, but the watery waving of a flashlight near the first cabin caught his attention. He hurried forward and saw Patrick's car parked in front of the row of cabins. The Irishman must have followed the police-man, Scott realized, and Patrick had already started to warn everyone.

Two figures came through the rain toward him, and Scott saw that Patrick had already alerted Barry.

"I'll pull the bus 'round front so the kids can load quickly," Barry shouted against the wind and took off at a run.

Patrick reached Scott and yelled in his ear, "Allie's getting Cabin One. The Tomlins have the next two. You take Four, and I'll get the rest."

"Right," Scott said and headed down the row of cabins. Around him, he saw frightened children, roused from their sleep, crying and turning deaf ears to orders to leave everything and get on the bus.

Allie grabbed up blankets as she prepared to herd five little girls out into the storm who had hastily dressed in the first clothes they could grab. Cathy seemed to be the least frightened of the group and had taken time to put in her hearing aids. Allie wasn't sure how much of the crisis she had heard or understood.

"Let's go! Hold hands! And stay close," Allie ordered as they left the shelter of the cabin, and started toward the milky lights of the parked bus.

Some of the little girls began to cry and wouldn't move unless Allie kept at their backs, shoving them forward. Her own heart caught in her throat when a flash of lightning showed her an engorged river spreading its waters only a few yards away from the center of the camp.

"Dear God, help us!" she prayed as she tried to hurry the terrified children through the drenching downpour.

Bob Tomlin was at the door of the bus, and he helped get Allie's group inside. Barry was in the driver's seat, the engine running, waiting for the signal that everyone was aboard.

Allie ran back to the next cabin where Marie Tomlin had her hands full with Randy's group of boys. In spite of orders to leave everything behind, the kids were grabbing clothes, suitcases and backpacks.

Allie saw that with his usual stubbornness, Randy had ignored orders and thrown on his jeans, shirt and jacket, and even put on socks and shoes. The backpack that he'd hid under his bed was now slung over his narrow shoulders stuffed with things he refused to leave. There wasn't time to argue with him.

"Let's go! The bus is waiting! Move," Allie ordered.

Randy bounded out of the cabin with the rest of the boys, and in contrast to Allie's group of girls,

Allie and Mrs. Tomlin didn't have to urge this group to run. They had trouble keeping up with them.

"Is that everybody?" Marie gasped when they reached the bus and got the last boy aboard.

"I know that Cabins One and Two are empty," Allie told her.

"What about the others?"

"I'll check. You get on the bus with the kids."

She had just started away when Trudy called out to her as she came running toward the bus with a couple of stragglers in hand. "Allie, where are you going?"

"To see if Patrick needs help. Have you seen Lily?"

Trudy shouted, "No."

"Check on the bus. See if she's there," Allie yelled against the tumult of the storm. "I'll double-check her cabin."

Trudy nodded and climbed aboard.

As fast as she could, Allie headed toward Lily's cabin. Blinded by assaulting rain, she felt as if she were fighting her way through a watery wind tunnel. She was so surrounded by murky darkness that she didn't see Scott until she nearly ran into him and a cluster of children he was hurrying toward the bus.

She bumped against him, and gasped with surprise, "Scott. I didn't see you."

"Where are you going?" he yelled at her. "Get on the bus. We've got only a few minutes to get out of here."

"What about Lily's cabin?" she gasped, trying to keep soaked tendrils of hair out of her eyes.

"Already evacuated. Patrick took her with him in his truck. There's no one left."

He grabbed her arm. "Let's get these kids on the bus and then you can get out of here." In a couple of minutes the camp would be empty. Good, he thought. He still had time to run back to the house, determined that he would save some important things from his desk.

When they had loaded the last of the children and Allie was about to board, he said, "I'll take the Rover and follow the bus."

"Hurry," she urged.

"I will." He turned to leave just as Randy came bounding down the steps and raced past them before either Scott or Allie had a chance to grab his arm.

"Cathy's not on the bus," Randy shouted back, and disappeared into the watery darkness.

"Randy, come back!" Allie cried.

Scott took in the situation and ordered Allie, "You get on the bus." He pushed her toward the first step. Barry was ready to close the doors. "I'll bring the two kids with me in the Rover."

She pulled away from him. "No, I'll stay." She wasn't about to leave Cathy and Randy behind. "Go, Barry. Don't wait."

A second later the bus door slammed shut and Barry gunned the engine. The heavy wheels of the bus sought for traction in the watery mud, and slowly began to move forward toward the wide planked bridge spanning the swollen river. In the next moment the taillight of the bus disappeared as it lumbered across the water-soaked boards. Floating debris was already collecting from high waters spilling over the guardrail onto the bridge.

"Randy! Randy!" Allie shouted and started running after the boy with Scott at her heels. Where would Randy go to look for Cathy? Maybe he was headed back to her assigned cabin, the one Allie had evacuated herself. Allie knew that the little girl had been with the others when she'd escorted them to the bus, and had left Cathy in the line of children climbing into the bus. Probably the little girl had run back to get something she didn't want to leave. But what? Allie knew she had remembered to put in her hearing aids. The little girl must have pulled out of the line and slipped away in the mounting confusion.

Scott felt as if he were caught in some kind of diabolical nightmare. Just as he thought the evacuation was under control, the whole thing had blown up in his face. In a few minutes more the wall of water boxed in by the canyon would reach the camp. They had to get out and get out now!

Scott yelled at Allie as he kept pace beside her in the downpour. "Where do we look?"

"Cathy's cabin," she called back. What if neither of them were there? Her mind shut down and wouldn't offer any help. They had to be there!

Her prayer seemed to be answered when they reached the cabin just as Randy was coming out of the door.

"Randy," Allie breathed in relief.

"Cathy's not here!" His voice was hysterical with panic. "Cathy's not here. I looked under the beds, everywhere. We've got to find her. She can't hear. She can't hear. She can't—''

Scott grabbed him by the shoulders and gave him a hard shake. "Randy, we don't have time to waste. Where would she go? Think!''

"I don't know. I don't know,'' he blubbered.

Scott despaired that searching the camp would be nearly impossible. The night was like a tunnel of darkness with driving sheets of rain and a lowering black-cloud ceiling. He also knew that he had little chance of getting Allie to leave without the little girl so he led the way down the steps of the cabin and out into the growing fury of the storm.

Allie grabbed Randy's hand and held it tightly. She wasn't going to take a chance of losing him again. Where was Cathy? Allie's stomach took a sickening plunge. She'd promised the Crawfords that she would take care of their daughter. The little girl could be anywhere in the darkness, crying out to them, and they would never hear her above the thundering, roaring tumult. She could have tried to get back to the cabin and become disoriented. In the driving rain, she could have started walking toward the swollen river instead of away from the flooding waters.

Please, God, help us find her. Allie couldn't believe that a few hours ago they had been enjoying music, laughter and fun. She remembered how Cathy's face had been aglow with— Her thoughts jerked to a stop. Cathy had been part of a group acting out nursery rhymes. She had been Little Miss Muffet looking at a book when the spider came up and sat down beside her. There had been a stack of books on her side—probably the same ones Randy had taken from the church. Books! Could it be—? Was this the divine guidance she'd been praying for?

"The activity hall!" she shouted to Scott. Keeping hold of Randy's hand, she turned in that direction. Maybe, just maybe, Cathy had left her books there after the show was over, and she went back to get them.

Scott didn't know what had put the conviction in Allie's voice, but the situation was desperate enough to follow her without argument. As he bounded up the wet steps of the wooden building ahead of her and Randy, he slipped and lost his balance.

He cried out as one leg went out from under him. Then, miraculously, he caught himself before landing with his full weight on either leg. The close call was sobering as he realized how near he'd come to spraining an ankle or even suffering a broken bone.

The front door to the building was open. As the three of them bounded inside, they could see a nightlight that Dorie had left on in the kitchen area, and a much brighter overhead light was spilling through an open door of the activity room.

"Cathy! Cathy!" cried Allie as they raced across the dining room, knowing full well that even if the little girl had had perfect hearing she wouldn't hear her name above the clamor of rain and thunder.

As they came charging through the doorway of the activity room, Allie gave a whoop of joy. Cathy was sitting on the floor, patiently putting books in a small box, and as they ran toward her, she greeted them with an innocent smile.

"Oh, Cathy," Allie blubbered in tearful relief.

"I got the books, Randy," she said, holding one up.

Scott grabbed it out of her hand and picked her up in his arms. "We're out of here! Let's go!"

Leading the way, holding Cathy firmly against his chest, he ran toward the door.

"Leave the books, Randy," Allie ordered as the boy picked up the small box of books.

The boy set his mouth in a stubborn line, and ran ahead of Allie, still holding the box as they left the building. Knowing it would be a waste of time to argue, Allie concentrated on trying to keep all of them together as they fought the storm again.

"This way!" Scott bent his head against the wind and led the way around the back of the building. He'd left his rented car at the back door of the house instead of trying to put it in his father's old garage that was so full of junk that even the old pickup would barely fit.

Under normal circumstances the back path to the house was a short one with a sloping hillside slanting down to the back door. Now the mountainside was like a giant rain gutter sending streams of muddy water over a slick, saturated ground.

How much time was left? The policeman had said about thirty minutes to evacuate, and Scott knew with sickening certainty that the escape window was closing with frightening swiftness. They had to get on the other side of the river, and drive out of the canyon without another moment's delay.

Weighted down with the little girl who was clinging to his neck with a stranglehold, Scott fought to keep from losing his footing on ground as slippery as a greased slide. Still hugging the box of books, Randy was right behind him, and Allie was in the rear, urging the boy to keep up with Scott's long stride.

As soon as they reached the car parked at the back of the house, he swung Cathy to the ground, opened the back door and shoved the two kids inside. Allie jumped into the passenger's seat and allowed herself a brief moment to lean her head back against the rest in thankfulness, as Scott started around the car to the driver's side.

Keys? He'd left the house in such haste after the policeman's alert, he couldn't remember if he'd picked up the keys. What if—? He shoved his hand into his jacket pocket. Not there! He'd long ago given up the idea that there would be time to save anything from the house, let alone go hunting for car keys. When his fingers clutched the metal key ring in his pants' pocket, relief was so physical, he felt almost weak.

He jerked open the driver's door, flung himself in under the wheel, started the engine and turned the windshield wipers on high.

Allie allowed herself a moment of thankful relief as she turned around and checked the two children in the back seat. Much to her surprise, they seemed oblivious to the danger that had threatened their very lives. Randy had dumped everything out of his backpack and was loading Cathy's books into it. Allie allowed herself a satisfied smile. Randy might be a handful, but his heart was in the right place.

They had just come around the side of the house, when the very earth began to shake with thunderous vibration. A new cacophony of roaring waters, splitting wood and rushing air rent the night with such force that even the heavy metal car seemed to vibrate. Scott slammed on the brakes.

"What's happening?" Allie cried.

He knew the answer. The wall of floodwaters that the policeman had warned him about was pouring into the canyon. Before their very eyes, a mountain of water began to rise just below them, spilling in threatening waves toward the house. They saw the splintered planks of the bridge tossed up like toothpicks in the rushing waters. The next instant the whole bridge was gone.

"Dear God," Allie breathed.

They could see that the cabins nearest the water were already being battered to pieces. Scott knew that once the force of the flood waters reached the driveway the car would be like a toy tossed into the floating debris.

"Out of the car!" Scott ordered. "We've got to climb to higher ground."

Allie and Scott opened the back doors and reached for the kids. With his usual stubbornness, Randy refused to leave his backpack, but there wasn't time to argue.

"This way!" Scott shouted. Waving his flashlight, he led the way back around the house where the southern side of Prospect Mountain sloped down to the garage and back door.

In the storm, the old mountain loomed cold, slippery and dark. Not an easy climb on a summer day, Scott knew. In the storm, footing on rocks, deadfall and saturated ground would be treacherous, but they had no choice. Climbing high enough to escape floodwaters rapidly rising between the canyon walls was their only hope of safety.

"Follow me closely," he ordered. "And step where I step." He was grateful that he knew the hillside behind the house as well as any kid knows the blocks in his neighborhood. During the summers they'd spent with their father, he and Jimmy had climbed over almost every ridge and promontory within hiking distance of the house. But with every precarious step, Scott realized a critical difference—he'd never been on Prospect Mountain in the blackout of a driving rain, and unable to see any kind of a patch beneath his feet. Every step they took on the shifting, waterlogged ground was a precarious one.

With the rising flood waters almost lapping at their feet, they scrambled upward as heavy rainwaters threatened to wash away the very ground beneath their feet. Allie cried out as a flat piece of sandstone gave way under her weight, crumbled and began to slide under her feet.

"Help!" she cried out as she let go of Cathy's hand, and reached out and grabbed the needled branch of a ponderosa pine which felt like a thousand pins sticking into her hand.

"Allie…Allie," Cathy wailed.

Struggling to regain her balance, she heard Scott yell, "Hold on!"

Blinking against the rain assaulting his face and

vision, Scott inched downward and struggled to keep
his own footing. He reached out his hand and she
grabbed it gratefully. Letting go of the tree, she was
able to move off of the broken rock and gain some
purchase beneath her feet that allowed her to regain
her balance.

"Okay?" he asked, putting his arm around her
waist when she was standing upright again.

She nodded, resisting the impulse to give in to the
temptation to shake her head no. She couldn't see
anything ahead or behind because of the thick drift
of trees that surrounded them. For all she knew, they
could be moving in a circle. "How much farther?"

"Not far," he lied. The truth would only discour-
age her. The short climb they'd made wouldn't begin
to put them out of the danger if the rainstorm was
still dumping rain in the high country. The high wall
of water could be sweeping half the hillside with it.

Allie grabbed Cathy's hand again, and Randy fell
in behind Scott. Sometimes the boy was bent nearly
double with the heavy backpack hanging on his
shoulders, but he doggedly kept at Scott's heels.

"I'm cold," Cathy whimpered.

"So am I," Randy joined in. "Why can't we find
a place to build a fire?"

Allie could tell that the boy's accusing tone blamed
Scott for keeping them in the drenching rain. With
childish stubbornness, he wanted things to be the way
he wanted them. The breath of tragedy that was so
nearly upon them had, obviously, completely escaped
him.

"Soon," Scott shouted back, his mind searching

furiously for any place on the mountain that would offer them shelter. The only place he could think of was a shelf of rocks halfway up the mountain slope that offered barely more than a hunched headroom under the rocky overhang. He remembered that he and Jimmy had cowered there one afternoon when a light rain surprised them. There certainly wasn't any room for a fire, but they'd be a little bit out of the downpour at least.

Scott was concentrating so hard on trying to keep his directions straight that he didn't realize that Randy wasn't still close behind him until the boy's voice floated up to him from some distance away. He swung his flashlight around and for a moment couldn't see any sign of the boy—or Allie and Cathy.

"Where are you?" he yelled, retracing a few of his steps. Then he glimpsed them in a huddle and realized that Randy had fallen spread-eagle on the ground. Allie was trying to help him back up, but weighed down by his backpack, the boy kept slipping back down in the mud.

When Scott reached them, he pulled Randy to his feet, and did what he should have done back at the car. He pulled off the backpack. He didn't know how the boy had managed to carry it up the mountain this far. "Get rid of it."

"No!" Randy lashed out at him, grabbing at the bag, trying to jerk it out of Scott's hand.

"It's too heavy for you to carry."

"No, no, it's mine, mine!"

There wasn't time to argue. Scott turned and threw

the heavy backpack down the hill with such force that it disappeared in an instant.

Randy screamed, "You—!" And he let loose a stream of profanity that included every bad word he'd ever heard in his tough little life. He started to lurch by Scott, intending to go after the bag, but Allie had him by the shoulders.

"Randy, stop it! Stop it!" She pulled the boy against her, holding him tight. "It's all right. It's all right."

As his little body pressed against hers, she realized that in his fury, and in the midst of his swearing, he was crying.

Cathy pressed against Scott's side, whimpering and shivering. "Carry me, carry me."

"All right. Get on my back," Scott ordered as he stooped down. "Put your arms around my neck. We'll go piggyback." Then he turned to Allie and Randy. "You two, stay right behind us. If you can't keep up, Randy, let me know."

Randy straightened his shoulders and Allie could almost see the fiery glint in the boy's eyes. "I'll keep up!"

She couldn't help but smile because Scott's words had exactly the reaction he had intended. As they continued their snail's pace through thick strands of aspen and pine trees, Scott's feeble flashlight began to flicker. No telling how old the batteries were. It would only be a few minutes before it went out completely.

"Pick up the pace," Scott ordered, but with the weight of Cathy on his back, he couldn't climb much faster and still be sure of his footing. Drifts of ponderosa pines and Engleman spruce grew thicker as they moved higher on the mountain, and overhanging branches served as a kind of canopy that shielded them from the full force of the downpour. This blessing was offset by the challenge of trying to keep a sense of direction in the dark cavern of trunks and branches.

Scott knew that every time they went around a mound of boulders or moved past a blockage of trees, his sense of direction was getting weaker and weaker. The hope that they were climbing toward the sheltering rock outcropping mocked their blind passage up the mountainside.

And then it happened. The flashlight went out.

For a paralyzing moment Scott just stood still. Only the dimmest contrast between the sky and trees gave any depth to their surroundings. In the enveloping shadows, he couldn't see to lead the way around fallen logs, rocks, trees or thick undergrowth.

Even as he turned to tell Allie and Randy that going on was impossible without having a light to show the way, the words died in his throat. The wind had blown darker and heavier thundering clouds overhead, and with them came a new peril within striking distance.

Lightning.

Allie and Cathy screamed as a blinding flash lit up the forest like the fluorescent lights on a football field. The strike couldn't have been more than a few hundred yards away. Stabbing desperation surged through Scott. No choice. They had to get in a clearing.

Don't stand under trees in a lightning storm.

"Hold hands, and don't turn loose," he ordered as Cathy clung to his back and Randy was positioned between Scott and Allie.

As a peal of thunder heralded each lightning strike, they stumbled forward in the midst of the thunder and forked flashes coming down from the dark sky. Although the clouds were moving farther away, several strikes were close enough to light up enough of the hillside that Scott was able to get his bearings.

He knew where they were! Scott gave an encouraging shout. "We're almost there."

They had almost reached the edge of the thick stand of conifers, just below the rocky outcropping that he had been seeking. When they stumbled out of the trees, no heavenly lantern could have been more welcoming as a sliver of moonlight breaking through the clouds and touching the rocky cliffs that stretched above them.

By the time they reached the narrow overhang just wide enough to shelter them, they had no reserves left. As they huddled together under the rock ledge, sheltered at last from the rain, Allie and Scott cradled the two children between them.

Physical exhaustion kept Allie from thinking beyond the moment. Tears of thankfulness blotted out nebulous stirrings that the nightmare might be far from over. They were safe from the floodwaters, and she clung to the faith that whatever happened next, a divine presence would look after them.

Scott wasn't under any such conviction. His own ability to cope was the only thing he trusted, and at the moment, he felt inadequate to the challenge of keeping Allie and the children safe. The responsibility that had been thrust upon him mocked his determination to remain free and unfettered. He couldn't even begin to think about what decisions would have to be made once it was daylight. What if the storm continued? How long could they cower under these rocks with two frightened children?

As the night passed, they slept fitfully. As soon as dawn began to lighten a wet, dusky, gray morning, Scott eased out from under the ledge, leaving Allie and the children huddled together in an exhausted sleep. The sky was still overcast, and a light drizzle was falling, but the dark, convoluted cumulonimbus clouds had moved on. There was a chance that the heavens might clear and allow the sun to dry out the drenched earth.

He shivered in the damp chill of a penetrating mist as he hiked a short distance away to a rocky point that overlooked the canyon below. As he stood there looking down on where the buildings of the camp had been, he wasn't prepared for the sight that met his eyes.

Chapter Nine

Scott's view from the high ridge on Prospect Mountain was devastating. Swollen waters of the river stretched from wall to wall of the canyon. The river's bank as it had been before had disappeared. All signs of the familiar places where he had sat beside the water and fished, or hiked along a wooded path skirting the river were gone.

He swallowed hard. Even though the crest of the flood must have passed, there was no sign that the water was retreating. Tumbled debris that might have been part of the buildings of the camp had been swept downstream or caught in rocks and tree roots exposed by the raging torrent.

Nothing remained of Rainbow Camp. Cabins, buildings and his father's house had been leveled by the water. Everything that had been the center of his father's life for so many years was gone. *Just the way you planned,* a stabbing voice reminded him. *Only Mother Nature did it for you.*

As he put his hand across his eyes, he struggled to get control of his emotions. Tired, cold and anxious, his usual commanding hold on reality wavered. He felt caught in some diabolic nightmare. They'd barely escaped when the bridge was swept away in front of his car. The scene had repeatedly flashed before his eyes in his fretful sleep. Every muscle in his body was stiff and aching from the hard climb and the burden of carrying Cathy up the steep incline. The total devastation that assaulted his eyes threatened to sap the last bit of reserve he had.

He didn't hear Allie's footsteps until she came up beside him. As he followed his gaze to the canyon below, he wished he could spare her the shock as she caught her breath.

"I don't believe it." Even though she'd seen news reports of floods and high waters, nothing had prepared her for the devastation that met her eyes. Magnificent tall trees had been uprooted; whole sections of bank had dropped away; and a wide expanse of roaring water was still eating away at the road. The scene was totally foreign to the quiet, awe-inspiring beauty of the mountain valley that had once been a haven of peace.

For a moment, total helplessness swept over her, but a wave of thankfulness almost instantly replaced the feeling. They were wet and cold, and alone on a rocky mountainside, but they were alive. They had escaped certain death in the raging storm, and whether Scott realized it or not, he had participated in a miracle. She prayed that others had been as blessed.

"What about the O'Tooles?" she asked, straining her eyes to try and see how far the water had reached up the opposite side of the mountain where they had their home.

"Oh, they're safe enough," Scott reassured her. "They built high enough to avoid any flooding from the river. Luckily Patrick drove out ahead of the bus so he didn't get caught like we did when the bridge went under."

"What about the main highway along the river?"

Scott tried to be upbeat. "If you're worried about the bus, they had a good fifteen-minute start on the crest of the flood. They should have been out of the canyon and away from the river before the road washed out." *Unless high waters had already eaten away sections of the highway,* he added silently.

Allie knew that they would have been on that bus if Cathy hadn't disappeared, and she blamed herself for not making sure that everyone in the line of girls got aboard. She'd left them on their own too soon, and now the Crawfords and Randy's foster parents would have to go through some agonizing moments when their children weren't on the bus. Thank heavens, Trudy had made it away safely with the others. Allie knew she'd be worried sick.

"I've heard about floods like this showing up about every hundred years in these mountain valleys," Scott said, shaking his head, "but I didn't know we were due for anything like this."

Allie hugged herself against the penetrating cold drizzle and gave him a weak smile. "I don't suppose there's a motel close by?"

He didn't respond to her levity. "There's nothing on this side of the mountain except rocky cliffs and trees, and more trees." He clenched his jaw. "We can't go down, and there's nothing above us but a small plateau before the ground drops off sharply on the northern side of this mountain."

She looked around at the continuous waves of mountain peaks that surrounded them in every direction. "Then I guess we'll have to stay here until someone rescues us."

At that moment, the sound of a childish whimper was carried on the wind. "Allie...Allie."

She turned and ran back to the rock ledge where two wide-eyed children were huddled against each other. Even though Allie and Scott had covered them with their coats, they were shivering.

"I...wa-want...to...go...ho-home," Cathy sobbed with chattering teeth.

"She's cold," Randy said, as if his own shivers were caused by something else.

"I know, I know." Allie scooted under the ledge beside them, and drew them both close. "But I think the sun is coming out, and we'll be able to dry off and get nice and warm again."

Scott heard her Pollyanna words, and they irritated him with their false optimism. The sun was not coming out! The rain wasn't stopping. Her hopes that the sun would come out were foolish fancy. If the dark clouds shrouding the high peaks were any indication, a new thunderstorm was brewing. What was worse, the wind was rising every minute.

Allie thought they could stay here until someone

rescued them. And how long would that be? And who would be doing the rescuing? No one could make it across the flooded canyon to climb up this mountain. He knew that it would be suicide to try and fly a copter in these narrow canyons, dashing any hopes that any news helicopters would be covering the scene. No telling how long it would be before they might be able to signal to an aircraft their presence in these rocky cliffs. In any case, there was no way to land a copter on the side of a hill, and the crest of Prospect Mountain was narrow and rocky. The mountain had gotten its name from early mining days when men prospected its slopes for silver and came up short. Scott and Jimmy had been all over this southern side of the mountain, and he knew that there was nothing that would provide them shelter while waiting to be rescued.

Randy pulled away from Allie's arms and joined Scott outside. "I'm hungry."

"Sorry, fellow. Breakfast is going to be late this morning."

Randy turned on his heels, and started to bolt away, but Scott managed to reach out and grabbed the edge of his jacket. "Whoa! And where do you think you're going?"

"To find my backpack."

"Forget it!" Steve ordered gruffly, putting his hands firmly on the boy's shoulders. "You're not going anywhere. Hear me? You're staying here. Use your head, Randy. What good would a backpack do?"

"We could eat the candy bars that I lifted from the

kitchen," Randy answered pugnaciously. "I was going to share them with Cathy. Now I can't." His little mouth quivered. "You threw them away."

"I'm sorry, really sorry, Randy," Scott said honestly, "but I'd rather have you safely here, even if we could have made good use of the candy bars. I was afraid that you were getting too tired to carry it."

"I wasn't tired. I just slipped in the mud."

"Randy, I need you to help keep up Cathy's spirits. Can you do that?" Scott asked.

"She's scared," he answered in a tone that spoke for both of them. "When are we going home?"

"I don't know, Randy, but I don't think we can stay here," Scott said, putting into words a growing conviction.

"Where we going?"

"I don't know."

"Bummer," Randy said as if that pretty much summed up everything.

Scott had to agree. He looked at the thickening clouds massing over the high western peaks. If they were going to make a move, it had better be quick, before the next wave of the storm made it impossible to seek out better shelter.

A cave would be a godsend, and allow them to get out of the weather, but as far as he knew there were none in this area. At least, he and Jimmy had never found one in their boyish explorations. One time they had hiked along the top rocky rim and looked down the other side where the ground dropped rapidly into an isolated canyon.

Isolated.

The word leaped at Scott like a firebrand. In his mind's eye, he was once again a young boy kicking at rocks in a game of sending them tumbling thousands of feet downward on the northern side of Prospect Mountain.

What if they land on that guy's roof? He could hear Jimmy's boyish voice asking the question as if it was yesterday.

What roof? I don't see any.

Down there. In those trees, Jimmy had insisted. *I think it's a cabin.*

You're seeing things. There's nothing down there.

Scott stiffened against the memory, afraid that a growing desperation was playing havoc with his thoughts. Had the conversation lingered in a forgotten corner of his mind all these years?

Was that the way it had happened? At the time, he had dismissed Jimmy's remarks without another thought. Had he recalled them now just to torture himself with the possibility that his brother really had seen the roof of the cabin within hiking distance of this rocky ledge?

Scott was afraid to trust his memory. As a quickening wind began to sharpen the rain pellets hitting his face, he knew that they had to move now, or continue to wait here, cold, hungry and at the mercy of another cloudburst that might loosen the rocks above their heads. Randy had gone back under the ledge, and he could hear Allie talking to the children in a soothing, promising tone.

"Allie," he called. "I need to talk with you."

"Okay. Just a minute." She took time to reassure

Cathy and Randy that she was going to stay close, and she'd be back in a minute. "What is it?" she asked, seeing the deep frown lines in his face.

"We have a decision to make." As succinctly as he could, he told her what the memory had been that had come to him. "I don't know if Jimmy mistook some rocks or trees for what looked like a roof one time when we were exploring. I know I didn't see anything. I could go check it out, but I don't think there's time to climb to the crest and get back before the next wave of the storm hits."

As a shock of damp hair blew across her face, she closed her eyes for a moment as she brushed it away.

"I can't promise anything, Allie," he warned her. "It's been years since that day. Even if there had been a cabin there, it could have tumbled down long ago. We could be worse off than we are now."

She straightened her shoulders and said, "Let's go."

"You're sure?"

She gave him a weak smile. "Why not see what's on the other side of the mountain? I don't care much for this side."

He smiled back and impulsively gave her a hug. "You're a real trooper. Remind me to award you a medal when this is all over."

"A gold one?" she teased as she drew away from the warmth of his arms.

"Absolutely." He turned to Randy and Cathy. "All right, gang. Let's move."

"We're going to find a nice cabin and get warm," Allie promised.

Scott cringed inside, knowing they would be more exposed to the storm than ever if they found nothing after a long hike but a hillside covered with rocks and conifer trees.

"Are we going to do some more climbing?" Allie asked, trying to ignore the ache in her stiff muscles.

"Not right away. I mean, we're going to stay at this elevation for a while," he told her. Deciding on the best way to reach the hoped-for cabin on the northern side of the mountain involved a calculated risk any way they went.

Scott knew the descent was too steep from the place where Jimmy may have glimpsed a roof below, even though that would have been the quickest way to reach the place. Going over the crest of the mountain and down the other side was just too risky.

He had decided that their best bet was a deep cut in the mountain that led to the northern side at about the elevation they were now. Once they hiked around to the back of the mountain, they would hopefully see the cabin, and then they would know whether to climb higher or go lower.

"Ready, troops?" Scott asked with as much enthusiasm as he could muster. Once again, Scott carried Cathy on his back as he led the way, and Allie held Randy's hand as they followed him.

The ground was as waterlogged and slippery as the night before, but the sodden dark sky allowed some diffused light from the hidden sun to play upon the mountain, and they could, at least, see where they were going.

As they wearily trudged forward, Allie silently repeated one of her favorite verses from Psalms. She knew that fear was the opposite of faith. Any anxiety about what would happen if Jimmy had only seen a mirage that day would be a betrayal of that faith. With that thought in mind, she firmed her trust in divine guidance as they trudged along a deep cut in the mountain. Sometimes they had to climb over mounds of fallen rocks that had tumbled down from above, and other times they could follow a natural path winding around the mountain as if mountain goats might have smoothed the ground for them.

When Allie glimpsed hardy wildflowers almost hidden in rock clefts she found renewed strength to keep putting one foot in front of the other. Lovely chiming bells with their clusters of tiny blue flowers glistening in the rain seemed to wave encouragement as she passed them.

Scott kept his eye on the sky and reluctantly called several rest stops as the morning wore on. He had no idea how far they had come or how much farther they had to go. Because the surrounding landscape was new to him, the perspective was entirely different. He knew that he could easily misjudge his location, and unless the hoped-for cabin was visible through the trees, they could hike right by it.

"It's a good thing we're high up," Allie said, as they looked down at the bottom of the draw where high waters were running fast in a wide stream that had already dislodged trees and bushes.

When they saw the half-submerged road snaking along the bottom of the ravine, he said grimly, "Nobody's going to be using that road for a while."

He didn't have to tell her what he was thinking. It was obvious that no rescuers would be traveling in this direction as long as the road was submerged. Luckily, they were able to stay high on the hillside, a safe distance away from the water.

The clouds were thickening overhead and the dreaded thunderclouds were forming. The drizzle had changed into a steady rain. Scott knew it was a race against time. If they didn't find shelter soon, they'd be caught in the same drenching downpour as the night before.

He was about to despair that there was any way to reach the northern side from the direction they'd been pursuing when his eye caught a glimpse of something red.

What was it?

As they hiked closer, he saw that the spokes of an old wagon wheel had been painted red and mounted in a mound of rocks. Scott asked himself why a decorative wagon wheel would be mounted like that unless someone who lived nearby had put it there?

Allie wanted to laugh and cry at the same time. What a welcome sign! In the dark, battering world around them, someone had left a touch of beauty, and like a beacon, it seemed to promise safe harbor.

They looked around but couldn't see anything but a thick stand of aspen and pine trees.

"It must be a marker," she said, pointing to a narrow path that disappeared into a forest of white-trunked aspen.

A clap of thunder sounded in the distance.

"Hurry," Scott urged and set a fast pace through

the trees. He was almost afraid to believe that sanctuary was near, but in spite of himself, hope sprang like a geyser.

"There it is," cried Allie as they broke out of the trees into a small clearing.

Facing them was a summer cabin made of logs, fashioned with a rock fireplace at one end and narrow redwood decks in front and back. A butane gas tank was next to the west wall, and a lightly graveled driveway led downward through the trees to connect to the submerged road below.

Scott allowed himself a silent cry of relief. *Bless you, Jimmy.* Randy gave a war whoop, and with the resiliency of youth, bounded forward. Allie's eyes filled with grateful tears that mingled with clinging droplets of rain easing down her cheeks as they ran to the front door.

"Down you go, honey," Scott said, quickly swinging the little girl from his shoulders. He began knocking on the door with demanding force.

Cathy whimpered as Allie drew her into her arms and tried to warm her shivering body. "It's all right, honey. We're going to get you dry and warm."

"Don't cry, Cathy," Randy coaxed in an unsteady tone that told Allie that the boy was trying not to give in to his own fears. "Maybe they'll have some of that hot chocolate stuff," he said hopefully.

"Hello? Hello? Open up." Even as Scott called out, he realized with sudden insight that no one was going to answer the door. On a day like this, the smell of wood smoke should have greeted them the minute they approached the house. No smoke had been coming out of the rock chimney.

No one was home.

He met Allie's eyes, and he knew she had come to the same realization. A warning rumble and the thickening pelting of rain forced his answer. "We break in."

Randy's eyes nearly popped out of his head. "Break in? But you said—"

"We don't have any choice," Scott said curtly, knowing that Randy was challenging his earlier lecture. He'd have to do some explaining later, but now, they had to get inside. "Any suggestions on how we do it, Randy?"

The boy hesitated for a moment as if this might be some kind of a trick to put the blame on him. Then he jutted out his little chin, and said, "Back doors are mostly the easiest."

Scott could see there was a double bolt on the front door, so he said, "All right. Let's give it a try."

Nearly blinded by the whipping wind and pelting rain, they made their way around to the back of the cabin. A rear door was set in the wall between high stacks of cut wood. Made of thick planks of wood, it was firmly locked, and didn't budge when Scott tried to put his weight against it.

"It'll have to be a window," he said, surveying the back of the house. Even before he had formed a plan, the shattering sound of glass jerked his head in Randy's direction. The boy had picked up one of the pieces of wood and hurled it through a window.

Both Scott and Allie were too dumbfounded to say

anything as he climbed up on the highest stack like a monkey, and began to clear out the jagged pieces of glass. Then he slipped through the broken window and disappeared inside.

A moment later the back door opened. A grinning, Randy motioned them in. "It's okay," he said. "Nobody's here. There's lots of good stuff around."

Scott and Allie exchanged smiles. Cold, wet and bone-weary, they went into the house together and closed the door against the perils that had brought them there.

Chapter Ten

As they walked through a small utility room and entered a dry, clean kitchen, the summer cabin was heaven come to earth. For a long moment they all just stood there, dripping water on a clean tile floor, shivering and trying to adjust to the blessed shelter from the pouring rain.

Their escape from the threatening elements had come so suddenly that Allie couldn't gather her wits. They had broken into somebody's house, and all the life-giving comforts that they had taken for granted were here. Obviously, the house was occupied. There were dishes drying in a rack, a book lay on the kitchen table and a couple of sweaters were tossed on a kitchen chair.

"Hello, hello," Scott called from a kitchen doorway leading into a long living room that stretched the width of the house. No one answered. Only the clatter of rain on the roof broke the silence. They trailed into the living room. The walls were brightly painted, decorated with pictures of flowers and kittens and the floor was covered with vibrant Indian rugs. It was a beautiful summer cottage, loved by someone.

"We need to get out of these wet clothes. It's all right, honey. We're safe now," she soothed to a whimpering Cathy. Then Allie shivered. "It's cold in here."

"If there's butane gas in the tank, we can turn on the wall heaters." He pointed to the gas panel in the living room. "And I'm betting there's hot water for baths." He smiled through raindrops dripping from his saturated hair and trailing down his cheeks.

"There's a box of matches by the stove," Randy offered, his quick eyes having already taken inventory of the kitchen. "I'm hungry," he said, eyeing the cupboards as if he could scarcely wait to rummage through them.

"First we have to get out of these wet clothes," Allie said firmly. Everything that they had on was encrusted with slimy mud.

"We ought to be able to find some warm things to put on," Scott agreed.

"Are we going to steal their clothes?" Randy asked in surprise.

"Borrow," Scott corrected.

Leaving a wet trail across the living room, they found the cabin had a nice-size bedroom and connecting bath. When Allie saw a baby crib in the corner of the bedroom with twin beds, her stomach took a sickening dip. "A baby!"

The missing family suddenly grabbed at her heart.

Where could they be? "Do you think they got caught in the flood?"

Scott didn't answer. He knew that any car traveling on the dirt road below the house would have been swept away in the rising torrent. There was bound to be loss of life in a flood like this one, but it wasn't going to do anybody good now to go into that scenario. He was still reeling from their narrow escape from the camp.

Allie's shoulders began to shake, and Scott realized that she was near a breaking point. How she had held up so gallantly this long in the cold, rain and physical exhaustion was astounding. He'd never known anyone with such dogged determination and faith. If she fell apart on him now, he couldn't blame her. He was about at the end of his own strength.

"Allie! See what you can find in the drawers and closets in the way of clothes," he ordered gruffly. He knew that he couldn't show any kind of weakness himself, or the others would pick it up.

She nodded, and went to the door of a small closet while Cathy and Randy stood shivering in the middle of the floor watching her.

"I'll check on hot water in the bathroom. You kids get out of those wet things now. We'll find you something to put on."

"I'm not wearing baby stuff," Randy said, exerting his usual pugnacious self. He looked like a stray who had stood under a rain gutter. His dark hair was plastered down, and his soaked jacket and jeans molded his tiny frame like wet paper.

What a kid. Scott couldn't help but admire the

boy's spunk. He was a handful, all right, but Scott would have chosen him over any other kid he knew to weather the kind of life-and-death experience they'd been through.

The closet revealed a variety of clothes for a woman, size sixteen. The lady of the house must be chubby, decided Allie. *The right size for Trudy,* she thought and suddenly foolish tears threatened to spill out of the corners of her eyes as she pulled some things off the hangers.

Allie had tried not to worry about her friend and the others aboard the bus. Scott had assured her that the bus had left the camp in time and had made it far enough down the main highway to be out of the flood area. *Please, God, let them be safe.*

"Hot water!" Scott said gleefully, coming out of the bathroom. "I've filled up a tub. You two gals are first. Don't argue," he warned as Allie opened her mouth to protest. Gently, he put a hand on her shoulder, looked into her eyes, and said softly, "I can't do this alone. Don't let me down now."

His touch nearly dissolved the last thread of resolve that lingered in her exhausted body. She wanted more than anything to turn and bury her face against his shoulder. How could she ever thank him for his courage and determination to bring them to safety?

"Hey." He lifted her trembling chin. "It's all right. Get a bath and put on some warm clothes."

Fighting a wave of total weakness, she took herself in hand as she looked at him. Mud stuck to his hair and face, and his clothes looked as if he'd rolled on the ground. Where was the stylish, young businessman with the smart haircut and the fashionable sportsman's attire?

"You look awful," she said with a weak smile.

"Really?" he said with mock surprise. He touched her nose and then showed her a dab of mud on his fingertip. She realized then that she must look as dirty and disheveled as he did. "Then we must be a matched pair."

As they smiled at each other, her spirits were strangely renewed. "Come on, Cathy. Let's get rid of all that mud."

After a quick bath, Allie put on one of the large woman's robes, and wrapped the little girl up in a large woolen sweater. While Scott and Randy took their turn in the bathroom, Allie tucked Cathy into one of the twin beds.

She kissed the little girl's forehead. "I'm going to find us something to eat," she said slowly so Cathy could read her lips. "Okay?"

Cathy nodded, closed her eyes and almost immediately her breathing told Allie that the exhausted child was already asleep. As Allie looked down at the fragile little girl, she couldn't imagine what anguish her parents must be going through at this moment. All the promises Allie made to them about camp being a wonderful experience for the delicate child rose up like specters to haunt her.

She could hear Scott and Randy in the bathroom, and wondered what they were talking about. She smiled, remembering how Randy had broken the window into the utility room and led them inside like Moses leading his people out of Egypt. The boy had no lack of courage, that was for sure, and his determination to save Cathy's books had nearly sent him tumbling down the slippery mountain. Allie knew somewhere under that tough veneer of his was a soft and vulnerable heart.

The robe that Allie had found to wear nearly went around her twice, and the bedroom slippers demanded a double pair of socks to stay on her feet, but she had never felt so wonderfully warm.

While Scott and Randy were bathing and dressing in clothes belonging to the missing man of the house, Allie went into the kitchen to see what she could find for a quick meal. It was mid-afternoon. They'd been fighting the storm, struggling to get here since nearly dawn. No wonder they were tired beyond belief and hungry as bears.

Standing for a moment in the middle of the kitchen floor, she looked around, grateful for a small, four-burner gas stove instead of a wood-burning stove. The few experiences that she'd had trying to cook on a cast-iron kitchen stove had usually ended up with a roomful of smoke and half-cooked food. When she saw a pretty kettle on the front gas burner, her immediate thought was hot tea. Thank goodness there was water in the house, probably piped in from a nearby spring, and all she had to do was find some tea.

She felt uncomfortable opening cupboards, and checking the contents of a small pantry. It was ridiculous but she had a foolish feeling that any minute someone was going to demand, "What do you think you're doing in my kitchen?"

A group of metal containers was lined up on pantry shelves. Opening some of them, she found coffee, tea, sugar, salt, flour, powdered milk and even a tin of cocoa which would make Randy's hopeful wish for hot chocolate come true.

She noted that all of the foodstuff that wasn't canned seemed to be kept in these closed containers, and when she saw a mousetrap in the corner of the pantry, she knew why. The knowledge wasn't comforting as she walked about in the too-big slippers.

When she looked around for a refrigerator, she realized with a start that there was no electricity in the house and the usual electrical appliances—toaster, coffee maker, can opener—were missing from the counters.

For a moment, she was put off-balance by the discovery. Life without electricity? No modern appliances? The covered box outside the kitchen window must be the only cooler, and the old-fashioned lantern hanging over the table was not just for show, but filled with oil. Since it was daylight, they hadn't tried to turn on a light, but now she realized that without electricity there would be no switches to turn on when it got dark.

Used to her compact little kitchen, even as she started to lament the absence of electricity, she was suddenly ashamed of how soon she'd forgotten to count her blessings. They had shelter, warmth, running water and food.

When the kettle began to sing, she made herself a large mug of hot tea and bowed her head in a moment of thankfulness. They had found their way through the storm and treacherous terrain by some miracle to this haven of safety. Blustery winds and rains continued to lash the windows like crazed beasts trying to get in, and she was grateful for the sturdy walls of the cabin.

When Scott and Randy came into the kitchen, she tried not to laugh. "You fellows look...warm."

"Is that all you have to say about our attire?" Scott teased, pushing out the middle of a pair of overalls big enough to contain two pillows. He wore a red flannel shirt that would have been roomy on a chubby Santa Claus. The slippers on his feet were large enough to be clown shoes, and the overall's pant legs were rolled up double.

Allie couldn't help it. She covered her mouth and laughed, and Scott's mouth spread in a grin. All the horror they had endured faded for a moment as they enjoyed a moment of shared laughter.

As for Randy, Allie thought he looked like one of the dwarfs in the *Snow White* movie. The wool shirt he wore dragged on the ground, and the too-long sleeves hung down his arms, completely covering his hands. He had a man's tie tied around his waist for a belt, and the woolen socks on his feet flapped as he walked.

"Ain't funny," Randy said in response to Allie's grin. He was like a porcupine ready to take on anyone who laughed at him. "I want my own clothes."

"Sure you do, honey," Allie said quickly. "You can have them as soon as we get them washed and dried."

"That'll be a challenge," Scott said. "No electricity. No washing machine."

"I guess we'll have to wash everything out by hand."

Scott frowned as he remembered something he'd seen as they'd walked through the utility room where Randy had broken the window. He left the kitchen, went into the utility room and came back carrying a tub and old-fashioned washboard, looking like a warrior returning with loot. "There's also a hand wringer, and a clothesline with some washing already hung up. Everything is wet, and the only thing I had to block the broken window was a piece of cardboard."

Randy lowered his head as if he were going to get bawled out for breaking the window.

Seeing the boy's reaction, Scott said quickly, "That was good work, Randy, getting us inside. You chose the right window to break. It doesn't matter about the utility room getting wet."

"It doesn't?" Randy blinked as if he wasn't hearing right.

"Nope. We'll pay for the window, and explain why we had to get inside."

"What if they bring the cops on us?"

"They won't. We're not here to steal."

"But we're gonna eat their stuff, and wear their clothes."

Allie hid a smile as Scott tried to explain why the circumstances made it all right to break into someone else's house, and use what they needed. Leave it to Randy to call a spade a spade. In his young mind, there was little difference between stealing and in helping themselves to everything they wanted.

"We'll reimburse them for everything," Scott assured the boy.

"What's that? Re...burse?"

"Reimbursing means to pay for everything you use."

Randy thought for a moment, scowled down at the enveloping woolen shirt that was hanging on him more like a tunic than anything. Then he looked up at Scott and said flatly, "I ain't paying."

Allie laughed aloud.

"Don't worry about it, kid," Scott said giving the boy's shoulders a reassuring squeeze. "Right now we're going to eat, sleep and wait out the storm as guests of these very nice people."

"Guess what, Randy?" Allie said brightly. "I've got the fixings for some hot chocolate. And there's canned soup. Chicken and noodle. How about that?"

He nodded, but was too tired to show much enthusiasm. A worried frown crossed his little face. "Cathy?"

"She's fine. After she has a nap, she'll be ready to eat, too. We'll take her some hot soup and she'll feel a lot better."

Scott gathered up all their muddy clothes and put them in the tub to soak while Allie heated up the soup and opened a box of crackers. Never had a simple meal seemed so scrumptious. As soon as they'd eaten, Allie took a bowl of soup into the bedroom and tried to get Cathy to eat some without much success.

The exhausting ordeal had taken everything out of

the little girl, and Allie couldn't rouse her enough to get more than a few spoonfuls down her. After getting the child to drink a little water, she gave up trying to get any nourishment down her.

Heavenly Father, keep her well, Allie prayed as she tucked the covers closely around her tiny body. The child was just tired, that was all. She needed sleep more than she needed food. When she woke up, she'd probably be fine.

Randy came in and when he eyed the nearly full bowl of soup, he scowled. "Why isn't she eating?"

"She's just tired," Allie reassured him. "And it's time you took a good, long nap yourself." She quickly turned down the covers on the other twin bed. "Say a prayer to God for bringing us safely here, and then get some sleep."

He climbed in and pulled the covers up high around his neck. It was obvious that he was completely worn out, and she didn't know how he'd managed to keep up with them during the hard climbs and the long hike.

As she tucked the covers in around him, impulsively, she leaned down and kissed his forehead. "Sleep tight. Don't let the bedbugs bite."

His eyes widened. "You mean this bed's got them bugs?"

"No, it's just a funny saying," she assured him.

He looked puzzled. "What's funny about bedbugs?"

"Nothing. Nothing, at all." She'd forgotten that she was speaking to a boy of the streets. No telling what kind of places he slept in when he was running loose, and the homey saying was serious business to him. "Don't worry, Randy. This is a nice clean bed, and you're going to have a wonderful sleep."

"Are we staying here?"

"Yes, for the moment."

"What if they come home and kick us out?"

Allie looked at the baby crib and her heart tightened. The road to the house was buried under water and muck. No telling when the owners had fled their summer cottage. Until the storm was over, they wouldn't know if they were coming back—ever.

"We're going to stay here until it's safe to leave," she reassured him. "Now, don't worry. Scott and I will be out in the other room if you or Cathy need us. Okay?"

"Okay," he mumbled. Then he flounced over on his side, and gave Cathy one last look before closing his eyes.

When Allie returned to the living room, she saw that Scott was kneeling in front of the fireplace. A small wood basket had been generously filled, and he was laying a fire.

The small gas heaters in each room had taken off the chill, but the living room stretched across the front of the house, and had two large windows exposed to the weather outside. An overhang on the deck gave some protection to the large panes of glass, and the storm was not as fierce as the night before, but rain still fell in sheets and plummeted loudly against the roof.

"I thought we'd fix you a bed on the couch, and I'll stretch out on the rug in front of the fire," Scott told her as he took a box of matches from the mantel, knelt down and coaxed the pieces of firewood into flame.

Allie looked at the small, floral sofa with its soft cushions, and decided it was the most beautiful thing she'd ever seen. A heavy hand-crocheted afghan was folded neatly at one end, and a couple of small pillows beckoned her weary head. Even though she didn't feel right about taking the last bed in the house, she was so bone-tired that she couldn't find the words to protest.

Scott turned around, and one look told him she was wavering on her feet. He quickly moved to her side, and he eased her down on the couch. Then he lifted her feet, and set her back on the pillows. "Time for a little R and R. You've earned it, lady." Then he took the afghan and spread it over her the way she had tucked in the children just moments before. "Stuck in this cabin with two kids for who-knows-how-long will wear better if we're rested. You better sleep the clock around if you can. Don't argue," he said as she opened her mouth to say something. He knew she was going to protest taking the sofa.

Weary lines creased her lovely face, and her mouth trembled slightly as she looked up at him. He smoothed back tousled blond strands from her forehead, and for a brief moment he fought the urge to take her in his arms and hold her. This was all his fault. If he hadn't given in and agreed to have the church camp, none of this would have happened.

"Get some sleep," he ordered gruffly.

"Scott," she murmured as her heavy eyelids threatened to close. "Thank you."

"For what?"

"For being you," she said simply, and closed her eyes. Almost immediately, her breathing deepened to an exhausted sleep.

Her childlike gratitude stunned him, and for some reason made him angry. How could she still be so innocent and blind? Why was she still looking at him through those adolescent glasses?

He turned away from the sofa and lay down in front of the fire, covering himself with an army blanket he'd found. As he stared into the red flames licking the wood and dancing in wild abandonment, he realized that Allie was still clinging to beliefs that had no relevancy when it came to survival in the real world. She'd escaped the harsh reality of what life was really about, but he'd experienced the truth firsthand when he'd looked on the bullet-ridden body of his brother. Even now the pain was still there, and the anger, too.

If only she hadn't walked back into his life again, none of this would have happened. He would have disposed of the property as planned, and no one would have been in danger of losing their life.

One thing was certain, dredging up old memories by coming back to his father's house had been a big mistake. Letting himself be drawn back into Allie's life might have been a bigger one. He'd known from the moment he saw her again that he should be listening to his common sense, instead of letting his emotions get the best of him. Life had taken them down different paths and even in this life-and-death situation, they were really strangers to each other.

As he listened to her even breathing, he knew that he would never forget her courage, her dogged determination, and the selfless giving of herself from the moment they'd fled the flood. If he'd doubted her stamina in the face of peril, she had proved herself over and above what he would have expected from anyone. It was too late to think about what might have happened if life hadn't taken them in different directions.

He was too tired to even think about what effect the flood would have on selling the property. One thing was certain, he didn't have to worry about leveling the buildings of the camp, but whether the prospective buyer would still want the land was another thing. At the moment, all he wanted to do was to go back to California, tend to business and put this whole nightmare out of his mind.

Chapter Eleven

When Allie awoke, she realized immediately that the force of the storm had slackened. Only a faint patter of rain sounded on the roof. Winds that had been whipping around the cabin had died down. The front room was in shadows except for the glow of the fire and a lantern light spilling through the open door of the kitchen at the other end of the room.

For a long moment, she just lay there, trying to orient herself and keep from groaning as she moved. She had no idea what time it was, the light was too feeble for her to see her watch, and lifting her arm up seemed like too much effort, anyway.

What did it matter? Her thoughts stalled. Her mind seemed unwilling to sort out a kaleidoscope of sensations. A perilous struggle for survival had obliterated all normalcy. Minutes, hours and days had lost their continuity. She was suspended in a kind of limbo until a murmur of Scott's voice broke through the detached floating state.

Her thoughts began to clear. Scott? She turned her head and saw that he was no longer stretched out on the rug in front of the fire.

Was everything all right?

Why was he up? Was he tending to one of the children? Cathy? Was she ill? A demanding urgency replaced the lassitude in her body. As she threw her legs over the side of the sofa, she wrapped the too-large robe around her, hurried in stocking feet across the living room toward the kitchen where Scott was talking.

As she looked through the doorway, she stopped and blinked. Was she awake? Or dreaming? A radius of lamplight shone brightly over the table and highlighted a scene that had nothing to do with the anxious beating of her heart and sweaty palms.

Scott, still wearing those ridiculous clownlike overalls, was holding a coffee mug in his hand. Cathy sat at the table in front of a bowl of cereal, and was grinning at Scott with a milk mustache.

"This is very good," she said as if it was the best breakfast she'd ever eaten.

"Eat up, honey. We've got plenty of powdered milk and two boxes of cereal. Oh, good morning," he said as he caught sight of Allie. "Come in and have a chair. The chef is ready to serve breakfast. Would you like a menu, or would you care for the specialty of the house?"

His levity almost brought tears to her eyes. She'd been prepared for another crisis, and his greeting was like a reassuring hug. She felt concern ease away, and she managed to respond in a light tone, "I'll take the specialty."

Cathy gave Allie one of her milk-mouth grins. "It's yummy. Just like the kind we have at home," she said and then went back to spooning up cereal as fast as her little hands could move.

Allie stopped at her chair and gave the child a light kiss on the cheek. "Good morning, sweetheart." Cathy was okay. She'd just been exhausted, not ill. Then Allie glanced out of the shadowy window. "It is morning, isn't it?"

"About five o'clock," Scott said, picking up a campfire coffeepot from off the small gas stove.

"Five o'clock? You mean I've slept ten hours?"

"Looks that way. I guess you were tired or something," he teased.

"Just a little. What about you?"

"Naw," he lied, knowing that he'd been ten fathoms down when Cathy's fretful cry jerked him awake. "Cathy woke up hungry. I guess you didn't hear her."

"No, I'm sorry. What about Randy?"

"He's still asleep."

She sat down in a chair opposite Cathy and stifled a groan as every muscle in her body protested the lightest movement.

"A little stiff, are we? I guess we ought to cancel any more hikes for a few days."

She eyed him frankly. "Don't give me any of that macho stuff. I bet your muscles are as sore as mine." Even though he obviously was in good physical condition, she didn't know how he'd managed to carry

Cathy all that way on his back. She felt guilty that he was the one who had gotten up and taken care of Cathy while she slept.

"Well, I'll admit I'm not up to running a marathon today." He glanced out the window. "The clouds are thinning. Maybe we'll get some clearing."

"I hope so." A large dose of sunshine would make everything look better. It was anybody's guess how long they would be here. At the moment, there was no way for anyone to reach the cabin unless they made the same grueling hike over the mountain. No telling how long it would be before the road was passable.

Scott set down a coffee mug in front of her. "You've heard about coffee strong enough to melt the cup? Well, here's your chance to try some."

She sighed. "The stronger the better."

"I think you're going to regret those words," he warned her. "I'm used to a percolator, not one of these campfire coffee pots." He filled a cup for her.

Allie turned toward Cathy, speaking loudly. "How you doing, honey?"

No answer. The little girl didn't even turn in her direction. Obviously, she hadn't heard Allie speaking to her. Allie shot a quick look at Scott. "Has Cathy been hearing you?"

"I guess so, although our conversation hasn't been a give-and-take. Why?"

"One of the morning routines at camp was to replace the batteries in Cathy's hearing aids."

"Oh, oh. That's not good," he said. The batteries

were gone. Swept away like everything else. "Can't she hear anything without them?"

"Only loud vibrations," Allie answered. Even though Cathy's lip-reading skills were improving, the child was dependent upon her hearing aids for even limited communication. Without them her significant hearing loss made her almost totally deaf.

Allie leaned across the table and touched Cathy's arm to get her attention. Then Allie lowered her head so the little girl couldn't read her lips. "Is the cereal good, Cathy?"

No response.

"Can you hear what I'm saying to you, Cathy?"

Still no response.

When Allie looked up, the child seemed puzzled and pointed to her ears. Then very carefully, Cathy took out the small hearing aids, which were fashioned with added receivers that went behind her ear.

"Here," she said as she handed them to Allie with the confident air of a child who expected the morning routine to be as usual. Allie looked at the dead hearing aids in her hands and wondered how she was going to tell Cathy that her link to the hearing world was gone.

Scott admitted that he hadn't paid much attention to whether or not Cathy was hearing him. "When she told me she was hungry, that took care of any need for further conversation."

As they talked about her, Cathy might as well have been in the next room. "Even a clap of thunder would be muted," Allie explained. "And even with her hearing aids, she's shut out of normal conversations. And without them—'' Allie's voice faltered.

''Without them, she'll get some practice in lip reading,'' Scott said evenly. ''A few days without her hearing aids isn't going to make that much difference.''

''But I promised her folks that I'd take good care of her,'' Allie protested. ''I convinced them that camp would be a wonderful experience for her.''

''Welcome to the real world, Allie. I guess it's time you learned that Pollyanna promises are so much wasted breath. They don't mean a thing,'' Scott said with a bitter edge to his voice. ''Thinking there's any rhyme or reason to any of this is just brainwashing.''

''I'm surprised to hear you say that, Scott. Especially since we're sitting here, safe and sound, drinking this horrible coffee. I suppose you think it was just a coincidence that you remembered Jimmy's remark about seeing the roof of this cabin that day on your boyish hike?''

''What else?''

''I don't believe in coincidences. I believe in divine guidance. You may not have been praying, but I was. And my prayers were answered. We escaped the flood by a miraculous few minutes, survived a night out in the storm and found our way here. And I thank God for it!''

He shrugged. ''If that makes you feel better, go for it. I've learned that what you can see, touch and get for yourself is all the truth there is. We're here because we had the strength and stamina to survive.''

''Scott, all those qualities you are so proud of came

from somewhere. We're the expression of something greater than we are. You're not going to tell me that you created yourself, are you? I know what grief is. When I lost my parents, I drew on God's promise that there is a purpose for everything that happens on earth and in heaven.''

"Allie, whatever you want to believe is fine with me. I've been down that patch and I found out it's not for me.''

"You got lost, that's all,'' she said stubbornly. "Maybe you need some different sign posts.''

"Well, I'll grant you one thing. Never argue with a woman on an empty stomach. Pass me the milk.''

Even though he had deftly changed the subject, she wasn't discouraged. Maybe she could find a crack in that hard shell of his in spite of his defenses.

After breakfast, they tackled the washing. Randy came in and ate breakfast while Scott and Allie took turns rubbing the soiled garments on the washing board before rinsing them in a tub. As soon as the boy had finished eating his cereal, Scott motioned him over to the hand wringer.

"See how this works Randy? You put the garment between the rollers and then turn. The water squeezes out and drops in the tub. Got it?''

"Washing is woman's work,'' Randy said, as if he'd heard the saying often enough to make it his own.

"Really? Then I guess you won't mind if Allie just takes care of Cathy's and her things.'' Scott eyed the too-big shirt hanging on Randy. "I guess you won't mind wearing that till we can get you home.''

"Bummer," he muttered, but took his place beside the hand wringer. When Allie and Scott handed him a washed garment, he inserted it between the rollers and turned the crank.

When Cathy came over to watch Allie scrubbing a pair of jeans on the washboard, Randy turned around and said, "Come on, Cathy, you can help me. You can catch the things on the other side of the wringer as they come through the rollers."

The little girl didn't turn around so he repeated her name, "Cathy." Randy looked puzzled when she continued to ignore him. "Are you mad at me or something?" he demanded.

"Cathy's not wearing her hearing aids," Scott told him.

Randy scowled, and his tone accused Scott of gross negligence when he said, "She's supposed to wear them all the time, except for sleeping."

"I know, Randy, but the batteries ran down, and we don't have any to put in."

"But she can't hear without them!" Randy's voice rose in anxious protest. "What'll we do?"

"We can help her lip-read. And be patient when she doesn't understand. Now, if you want her to help you, let's show her how to help catch the clothes from the wringer. You'll have to be patient," he warned. "Okay?"

Randy nodded.

Scott touched Cathy on the shoulder, and with mimed gestures told her that he wanted her to stand on the opposite side of the wringer. Then he had

Randy put a garment through the roller and showed the little girl how to catch it and put it on the counter.

He waited until they had run a couple of things through, then he nodded and gave Cathy and Randy a smile of approval. Good kids, he thought. He hated to think how two spoiled kids could have added to trauma. Neither Cathy nor Randy had made things difficult. Allie and he were lucky that they were good troopers, both of them.

"I'm going to string a clothesline in the living room instead of the utility room so they'll dry quicker," he told Allie.

"A good idea," she said, pretending that she hadn't seen what had gone on between him and the children. The way he'd handled both Randy and Cathy showed that he hadn't lost his knack for working with kids, even though she knew he'd be the first to deny it. That summer they'd been youth counselors, she'd watched him relate to their young campers with patience and ingenuity. Maybe this forced opportunity to renew those skills would revive some of the old joys and give him a different perspective of himself.

When the washing was done, all four of them proudly viewed the line of clothes strung across the living room. Scott had built up the fire in an effort to speed up the drying. The lovely smell of clean, wet clothes filled the air, and Allie was glad that the activity had been a team effort. She could see the pride on the children's faces, and even Scott's expression was one of satisfaction.

Later in the afternoon, her mouth fell open when

Randy made a sign with hands and Cathy nodded in agreement.

"I didn't know you knew sign language, Randy."

He shrugged. "A little bit. Cathy's supposed to be learning how to do it. She has a book that shows all kinds of signs. She's kinda lazy though," he complained in an older brother's tone.

"Well, maybe you can practice some of the signs you remember."

He brightened. "Yeah. I can do most of the alphabet, but I like whole words better. You don't have to know how to spell."

Scott chuckled. Smart kid, he thought. Randy might get his life in order if given the chance. His protective attachment to Cathy was unusual for someone who had been bounced around the way he had.

Cathy had been looking at each of them as Scott and Randy spoke and a frustrated expression creased her little face. Obviously, she was unable to understand what they were saying.

She tugged on Allie's hand and then pointed to her ears. "I need my hearing aids," she said. "Put some new batteries in them, please."

Suppressing a sigh, Allie drew Cathy over to the sofa. She spoke very slowly and formed her words with deliberate exaggeration as she faced the little girl. "I'm sorry. I don't have any batteries for your hearing aids." She shook her head and held out her empty hands. "The flood took them away. Understand?"

Cathy continued to stare at Allie's lips, as if waiting for some comprehension of what was being said.

Then she raised questioning eyes to Allie. "I need my hearing aids," she repeated, and there was a quiver of anxiety in her voice.

Allie took the hearing aids out of her pocket, and deliberately took out the dead batteries. Then she handed the hearing aids to Cathy and pointed to the empty spot where the batteries belonged, and shook her head. Holding out her empty hands, she shook her head again.

Cathy's face began to scrunch up in tearful understanding. "No batteries," she said. "No batteries."

Allie gathered her close, murmuring "I'm sorry, honey," even though she knew Cathy couldn't hear her.

Randy came over and sat down beside them. He tapped Cathy on the shoulder and made her look at him. "It's okay," he said as he formed "O" and "K" with his fingers, and then nodded his head. "Okay?"

A surprised look replaced Cathy's frown. Very carefully she followed his example, forming the same two letters with her own little fingers, and saying aloud, "O-K."

Allie and Scott exchanged smiles. She knew that the best thing to do was to leave the two children to build their own bridge of communication, so she left the living room and went into the kitchen. Scott followed.

Leaning against a counter, she said with relief, "One hurdle over. As long as Cathy can communicate with Randy, she'll be able to handle all of this, I think. It's surprising that she hasn't been crying for her mother. She's a lot tougher than I ever would have imagined.''

"Kids are resilient," he admitted. "We should be able to get them back home in one piece."

"When?"

"Well, not today, that's for sure." He peered out a window at the overcast sky. Lead-gray clouds still masked the morning sun and held the threat of more rain even though it had stopped during the night. "One thing's for sure, we're staying put. One of the first rules of staying safe is not to move around. There are hundreds of stories about people who get into trouble in the mountains and they never stay put so that someone can find them and come to their rescue."

"It should be clearing up soon," she said hopefully, refusing to give in to any speculation that the weather would remain the same as it had been for three days. "I wonder what the weather forecast is."

Scott looked puzzled. "Have you seen a portable radio anywhere?"

Allie thought for a moment and then shook her head. "No, I haven't, but I haven't been looking for one."

"That's funny, isn't it? I mean considering how well equipped this place is. Everything about the place has all the signs of a family settled in for the summer, at least. You'd think they'd have a radio, wouldn't you?"

"Maybe they don't want any contact with the outside world, and all its trouble. This could be a kind of retreat for them."

"Some retreat," he muttered, not wanting to think how permanent their retreat from the world might be. If the owners of the cabin had been listening to the radio, they might have stayed here where it was safe. "I think I'll double-check the bedroom."

Allie went back in the living room, and saw that the two children were still sitting on the sofa. It warmed her heart to hear them both giggling. She wasn't about to intrude on whatever was going on between them.

She had noticed an old bookcase at the opposite end of the room from the fireplace. Curious, she sat down on the floor and opened the glass doors. The shelves were filled with mostly old books.

As she looked them over, Allie decided that one of their absentee hosts must be a mystery buff from the number of whodunits on the shelf. There were numerous non-fiction books on the history of Colorado, and early days in the West. What pleased her most of all were two wonderful discoveries on the bottom shelf—a dusty Bible, and several well-worn children's books that were signed to a Ruth Thompson on various childhood birthdays from years past. Looking at the dates, Allie decided that they must belong to their absent hostess. Allie speculated that Ruth had grown up, married and now had a baby of her own. Once again, Allie's chest felt heavy thinking about the couple and their baby who might never come home again to enjoy the books that Ruth Thompson had saved in this old bookcase.

Allie opened the old Bible carefully, and turned to her favorite scripture—Psalm 91. The scripture verses had renewed meaning in the present circumstances, and she drew them to her heart. "Thou shalt not be afraid for the terror by night; nor for the arrow that flieth by day...he shall give his angels charge over thee, keep thee in all thy ways."

"Whatcha got, Allie?" Randy asked as he and Cathy ran across the room to where she was sitting in front of the bookcase.

"A surprise," she said, putting down the Bible and holding out the children's books. "Look what I found."

Cathy's eyes widened, and she looked at Allie as if she couldn't believe her eyes. Randy looked even more astounded, as if the ones they'd thrown away had suddenly materialized in front of his eyes.

"Books," Cathy said, and her little face glowed as she took a copy of stories by Hans Christian Anderson and handed it to Randy. "Ugly Duckling," she said, smiling.

"God provides, doesn't he?" Allie said casually. "Someone named Ruth left them here for us to enjoy. We'll handle them gently and then put them back where they belong, won't we?" Her smile was a warning to Randy. "Why don't you and Cathy sit in front of the fire and enjoy them? Cathy can look at the pictures, and read all but the hard words herself. Besides, she can get some practice lip-reading if you say the words slowly and then point to them on the page."

Randy looked thoughtful for a moment, and then nodded. "Okay, I'll be her teacher."

"Good." Allie nodded. "She needs someone older to help her."

"She likes me reading to her, don't you, Cathy?"

The little girl grinned at Randy without any indication that she understood what he had asked her, but it didn't matter. Anyone could see the answer to his question on her face.

Allie stayed sitting on the floor in front of the bookcase as they settled on the rug in front of the fireplace. With their backs to her, sitting side by side, the silhouette of two children made a tender picture as they bent their heads over one of the large books. Children were wonderful when it came to living in the moment. They seemed to be born with a natural trust and faith until the conditioning of the world replaced them with fear.

When Scott came back in the room, he sat down on the floor beside her. He saw the Bible in her hands but didn't say anything about it, and Allie knew better than to try and share the comfort that the scriptures had given her. How could you convince someone that the presence of God was everywhere when He appeared not to hear your needs?

"No sign of a radio," he told her. "I can't believe these folks lived here without one. Can you imagine sticking your head in the sand like an ostrich, and not knowing what's going on in the world? Without radio, television and newspapers, they're cut off from everything."

"Maybe that's why they chose this isolated cabin. They didn't want the world intruding."

"Maybe. But there are times when ignorance is a

heavy price to pay. This flood is a case in point. Of course, there wasn't much warning for anyone about the floodwaters,'' he admitted grimly. "But a radio would sure be a help now. How are we going to know when they start some rescue efforts?''

"What will they do first?'' And when? She couldn't bear to think about the anguish their loved ones must be going through, believing that all four of them had drowned. Scott had not mentioned his mother, but surely he was aware of the pain she must be enduring thinking her second son was gone. Allie knew that Madeline Davidson wasn't anything like Sam, but her dedication to Scott's welfare, however materialistic, was sincere. Allie's heart ached for any mother enduring the torment of not knowing what had happened to her child.

She knew that Randy's foster parents would be concerned about him, but there were no deep ties between them and the boy. In fact, Allie didn't expect Randy to stay long with them. The couple had already made noises about moving him. The Crawfords would be heartsick over their daughter, and then there was Trudy. Allie knew her dearest friend would be devastated. If only there was some way to tell everyone they were safe and sound.

"Surely they'll be checking all the cabins and summer homes as soon as the waters recede,'' Allie insisted.

"Most likely there'll be some helicopter flights as soon as the weather clears. If we can rig up some kind of a signal on the roof, we may be able to catch their attention. We're really on the wrong side of the mountain for them to be looking here first. I imagine they'll fly up and down the mountain canyon, checking it first before spanning out to wider territory.''

''Then it might be a few days,'' Allie said, trying not to let herself get uptight. After all, they were perfectly safe here, with all the conveniences of a home.

''What are the kids doing?'' Scott asked, hearing their childish voices and giggles.

''I found some children's books. Don't they make a sweet picture sitting there together?'' She sighed. ''It makes me wish I had some of my own.''

''I suspect you'll get around to it when you find Mr. Right. I'm not the fatherly type. I guess I take after my mother. She likes her independence, and always said that kids tie you down. When she and Dad divorced, she took Jimmy and me only because she believed that Dad would never make a decent living for us. She was right about that. I'd never have been able to afford college if it hadn't been for my mother.''

''You would have found a way,'' Allie told him. ''And your dad gave you a lot of things that didn't have a money tag on them. Remember how wonderful all the summers were that you spent with him? How can you put a price tag on that?''

''I suppose you're right,'' he admitted, ''but unfortunately we can't live in a kid's world forever.''

''We can try.''

''You can't be serious.'' He gave a short laugh. ''You really have been protected from the real world, haven't you?''

''No. I've had my share of challenges. But it was

a wise person who said that it isn't what happens to you that matters; it's how you let those things affect you."

"Sometimes we don't have a choice."

"We're not robots," she challenged.

He shook his head. "You always were an idealist, Allie. Why haven't you married and had a family if that's what you think life is all about?"

She was thoughtful for a moment. "I guess I've been waiting to fall in love with a man my soul could love."

He fell silent. What could he say? *A man my soul could love.* Her words completely disarmed him, and he couldn't bring himself to make light out of her admission. Her sincerity was without question. She would never marry lightly, nor hold back any of herself. The man who captured her heart would have to be someone worthy of that love. He swallowed hard. "You deserve the best, Allie. Don't settle for anything less."

"What about you, Scott? Don't you want to fall in love and get married?"

"No," he said flatly.

"Why not?"

"You ask too many questions, Allie. I know you mean well, but at the moment, my only concern is to get you and the kids back in one piece. Life will go on as it did before this happened. You'll go back to counseling and waiting for that soul mate to show up. I'll put all my energies into increasing my business and financial status, and that will be that." He rose to his feet. "While I was looking for the radio, I found something that might interest you."

"Oh, what's that?"

"Come on, I'll show you." He reached out, helped her to her feet and guided her into the kitchen.

When he pointed to the table, she started laughing. A checkerboard, complete with red and black checkers, was laid out for a game.

"As I recall, you owe me a game," he said solemnly, with a glint of amusement in his eyes.

"No, I beat you fair and square for the championship."

"You did not. My dad hemmed and hawed when you were about to make a mistake, and he guided you through every move. Sit down, my pet. Revenge is sweet."

They played three games. He skunked her every time. But she didn't mind. The softening lines in his face, the twinkle in his eyes and the way he teased her was worth every checker on the board.

Chapter Twelve

For the third day, Scott was isolated from a world of ringing telephones, demanding computers and financial decisions. He never would have believed it. In some ways he no longer felt like himself. All of the triggers for hurrying, working, striving and making each moment count were gone. He was surprised how easily he adapted to this forced hiatus from stress. If there had been anything he could do about business, he would have centered his energies on taking care of company matters, but without the means to carry out any decisions, he was able to put all financial cares on hold. He told himself that there would be time enough later to solve the problems that would undoubtedly be stacking up while he was away from the office.

The tiny summer cabin was so completely isolated from the world that it gave the illusion that nothing beyond the warmth and security of its walls existed, and for the moment, he was ready to believe it. He was content to watch Allie's tranquil face as she played with the children or just sat quietly, lost in quiet meditation. He found himself laughing with Cathy and Randy or lying in front of the fire as leaping flames mesmerized him with their playful dance.

Allie couldn't help but notice the change in him. At camp Scott had been distant, judgmental and impatient. He had separated himself from the Christian values that they once shared, and he could have gone back to California without their lives touching in any personal way. Instead, here they were, safe from the floodwaters, having time to talk and share feelings, and recapture the joy they'd found in each other in their youth. She knew beyond a doubt that under that hard, worldly veneer, Scott was still the tender, vulnerable young man who had stolen her heart once before.

"Why are you smiling?" he asked. They were sitting in the kitchen, enjoying a cup of tea while the children were down for a nap. "You look as if you're enjoying some kind of a secret."

"Maybe I am."

"I'll give you a nickel for it."

"Big spender," she teased. "I'll give you a dime if you guess it."

"Is it about me?"

"Yes."

As he looked at her, Scott suddenly stiffened. The loving tenderness in her eyes shot a warning through him. How easy it would have been to reach out and take her hand, and feel the warmth of her clasp radiating from the touch. He remembered how they had walked together, feeling the glow of young love as their eyes met. How wonderful and simple life had seemed then, holding hands, walking in the moonlight and sharing dreams. They'd never had a chance to deepen those first romantic feelings of boy-and-girl sweethearts, but she could still engage his feelings as no other woman ever had.

No, Allie, no. Don't look at me like that. Hurting her was the last thing in the world he wanted to do. Didn't she realize that the pattern of his life was already set? He'd come too far down a different road in the years they'd been apart. She had said she wanted a man her soul could love, and he knew better than anyone that he could never measure up to be the mate her faith demanded. He cared too much for her to belittle the spiritual fiber of her being by pretending to be something that he wasn't.

Allie saw the corners of his mouth tighten, and the companionship they'd been enjoying suddenly become strained. Was she revealing too much of her own feelings? What door had she opened that he was determined to keep closed? She didn't want him to read the truth that being here with him was close to being a dream come true.

For a short time after that halcyon summer, it had seemed that their adolescent love would blossom to a complete and meaningful life together. Before they drifted apart, she had fantasized about being with him like this, laughing and sharing, letting the rest of the world go by. She had been saddened that their lives had spun off in different directions. By the time they graduated from separate colleges and Scott had gone into business, the closeness between them had evaporated.

She had entertained a foolish hope that he echoed her own feelings of renewed closeness, but the closed look on his face told her that he was determined to keep an emotional distance between them. In spite of everything, he wasn't about to lower his guard. *Face it, Allie. He doesn't want you in his life again.*

"Some secrets are better kept, I guess," she said quickly and lowered her eyes.

He cleared his throat as if trying to find the right words and tone. "Allie, in a few days everything will be back to normal. All of this will seem unreal."

"It seems unreal now," she admitted.

If it had been any other woman but Allie, he might have lied and said he hoped they would stay in touch, but he couldn't play games with her. He had to face the truth. There was no place for her in his world.

"A life-and-death experience like this can never be forgotten," he told her, "but once we're back in the same daily grooves as before, nothing will have changed. Do you understand what I'm saying?"

"Let me guess. You're warning me not to make the mistake of thinking this experience has changed you in any way."

"I guess you could say that."

"Not even made a few cracks in that hard shell of yours?" She spoke brightly, not wanting him to know the depths of her feelings.

"Well, I wouldn't have put it exactly that way," he admitted with a wry smile. "But I guess that's close."

"Scott, I have to admire your tenacity in holding on to a lifestyle that doesn't fit you," she said frankly. "But you can't convince me that you haven't been more yourself since we entered this cabin than you've been in years. How long has it been since you've laughed, played with kids and beat someone at checkers?"

He shrugged. "When you're stranded away from the world and everybody in it, there's an unreal quality about everything." His eyes softened as he looked at her. "And as much as anyone might like, no one can stay stranded forever."

There was just the slightest hint of wishful thinking in his words that made Allie secretly hope that maybe he wasn't all that eager to get back to the rat race after all. She'd seen a softer side of him, a caring and giving side that didn't fit into the corporate world that he professed to want, but he was right about one thing. All of this would seem like a dream once they were back in their usual daily patterns.

"How much longer do you think we'll be here?" she asked, but he didn't answer.

She turned and looked out the window where lingering dark clouds were casting a gray, wet mantle on the wooded hillsides surrounding the cabin and a dark haze hid the high peaks from view. "I can't believe the rain has hung around this long. Just when it looks as if it's going to clear and the sun might come out, it clouds over again."

"I can't imagine what the streams and rivers look like—" He broke off as a loud blare of noise sounded through the house. "What was that?"

Allie couldn't identify the sound. Just noise. Almost like the shrill of a loud speaker. They jerked to their feet.

"I think it came from the bedroom," Scott said.

Had one of the kids screeched like that? Allie asked herself as they bounded out of the kitchen and across the living room to the bedroom door.

Throwing the door open, they saw that both Randy and Cathy were still in bed. The little girl was breathing heavily, eyes closed, and her arms and hands laying tranquilly outside the bedcovers. She was obviously sound asleep.

Randy was in his bed, lying with his back to the door, motionless except for a betraying movement of one foot under the covers.

Scott gave Allie a knowing nod. There was no way the boy could have slept through that noise. Randy's hearing was perfectly normal.

He was faking.

Scott walked around the bed and stood there quietly for a moment, looking down at the boy. When he saw a flicker of Randy's eyelids as he pretended sleep, Scott reached out and pulled the covers back with a quick jerk.

Randy sat up with a start, hugging a small radio.

Neither Allie nor Scott could believe their eyes.

"I found it. It's mine. Finders, keepers. Finders, keepers," he kept repeating.

"Oh, Randy," Allie moaned. "How could you?"

Scott's face grew red with fury, and he clenched his fists to keep from jerking the radio out of Randy's hands.

"I didn't mean to make a noise. I turned the wrong button." Randy looked at her anxiously, as if that was the worst of his doings.

"Didn't you know we were looking high and low for a radio?" Scott managed in a fairly normal tone, keeping his voice tightly under control. He didn't dare let loose with the fury he felt knowing that he'd been right about the improbability of the owners living here without a radio.

"It was right here by my bed when we got here." Randy glared back at him. "I took it when both of you were busy snitching clothes from the closet. It's real neat. I could have told you it was going to keep raining, if you'd asked me."

Allie was stunned. Randy had taken the radio the first hour they were in the house, and all this time they could have been listening to weather reports, news about the flood and information about the rescue efforts. She could see that Scott was ready to throttle the boy.

"Randy, you should have let us know about the radio," she said sternly.

"I kept it under my pillow," Randy said with a hint of pride that they hadn't found out about the radio until now. "Cathy knows I have it, but she can't hear the radio when I turn it on so it doesn't bother anyone."

"That's not the point, Randy," Allie said sharply. "We need to know when the weather will break and how soon someone will be looking for us."

"Give me the radio," Scott ordered, holding out

his hand. "I thought we'd had an understanding about taking things that don't belong to you."

"You guys are taking all kinds of stuff," Randy argued, continuing to clutch the radio with both hands.

Allie sighed. How could a ten-year-old boy who'd never had anything of his own understand the fine line between borrowing and stealing?

"Give Scott the radio, Randy," she ordered. "We'll talk about this later."

"I want it back," he said defiantly, reluctantly loosening his grip on the radio. "It's mine."

"No, it isn't yours," snapped Scott as he grabbed the radio. "It belongs in the house, and we're leaving it here. We'll take nothing that doesn't belong to us. Do you understand? And we'll leave enough money to cover the cost of everything we've used."

"What about the books?" he argued. "Cathy likes them."

"They stay."

"We could leave money for them, couldn't we?" he insisted.

"Randy, those books are special to someone," Allie answered firmly. "You and Cathy can enjoy them while we're here, but we can't steal them."

"Why can't we borrow them—and not bring them back?"

Scott turned to Allie, and with an exasperated shake of his head said, 'I give up."

He walked out of the room with the radio, leaving Allie to explain right from wrong to a belligerent little boy who wanted to make sure his little friend didn't have to give up her books—again.

Scott set the radio on the kitchen table and tried several stations before he found one that was fairly clear of static. Unfortunately, country music was the only thing they were broadcasting at the moment. Eager to get a weather report, he turned the dial on both frequencies, but was unable to pick up a second station.

Frustrated, he turned the radio off. No telling if Randy had run down the batteries while listening to the radio hidden under the bedcovers. That kid was something else. Sharp as they come and just as devious. Scott only hoped that someone would take enough interest in him to straighten him out before he got into real trouble.

Allie came into the kitchen with an expectant look on her face. "What did you find out?"

Scott shook his head. "Nothing. Only one station and it's cowboy music. Maybe we'll get something on the hour or half-hour."

"We're getting low on canned food," Allie said. "And there's only a little powdered milk left."

"Maybe we should think about going on rations." He glanced at the rain-spattered window. Even if the rain stopped tonight, he didn't know how long it would be before the road would be passable. It could be days before it was safe to leave or alert someone that they were here.

They sat in silence until Scott turned on the radio again. This time they were successful in getting the news and weather report. They listened to a broadcaster's report with growing concern. The whole canyon had been devastated by floodwaters, and the death toll was climbing. The one bit of good news was that the weather would be clearing by morning. Rescue helicopters would be flying over the area for the first time.

"We have to let them know we're here," Scott said, as he turned off the radio.

"How?"

He thought for a moment. "We need to put a sign on the roof. One that's big enough to see if any of the copters fly over the northern side of Prospect Mountain. I'm sure they'll be concentrating on the canyon area. We're out of the way for any rescue teams searching along the river. According to the radio, all the settlements upstream were washed out."

"Don't you think they'll fly all over the area, looking for survivors?"

"It's going to take time. If we were still on the southern side of Prospect Mountain—"

"Where we spent the first night? Under the rock ledge?"

"Right."

"Well, I'd rather be waiting to be rescued here, than there, even if it takes some extra days." She still couldn't believe the miracle that had led them to this safe refuge.

"I don't think there's much chance of the road around to this northern side being passable very soon," Scott said, "but if they do an aerial reconnaissance, we might be able to attract some attention with a sign. At least then, they'd know that we are here even if it is a while before they get to us.''

Allie didn't doubt for a minute that if someone knew they were here, help would not be long in coming. After all, if they had hiked to the cabin, she reasoned, someone else could do it, too.

Scott got up from the table. "We'll need some paint. Have you seen any around?"

"Maybe you should ask Randy," she said with a faint smile. "I doubt that there's much around that he hasn't already spied."

"True. I bet that little yahoo has been through every drawer and closet. We're going to have to frisk him before we leave here."

Allie agreed and made a mental note to make sure that Ruth's books were back in the bookcase, safe and sound. Randy seemed to have an obsession about Cathy and her books.

After Scott had searched the utility room and came up empty, he asked the boy if he'd seen any paint cans around.

At first Randy was suspicious that it was a trick to get him in more trouble. Allie had to convince him that they needed his help.

Before he would commit himself, Randy made up a big, long tale about hearing a mouse, and was looking for a broom to swat it when he accidentally saw a can of white paint sitting next to a tin of graham crackers at the back of the pantry.

Then he admitted sheepishly, "Me and Cathy ate the crackers...well, most of them. We still got some under her bed."

Allie suspected that Randy had a horde of food stashed away for him and Cathy. If anyone went on rations, it would be Scott and herself.

Scott found a paintbrush in the toolbox he'd brought in from the utility room. "Now all we need is a dark-colored sheet or blanket."

"Whatcha going to do with it?" asked Randy, ready to let bygones be bygones.

"I'm going to paint S.O.S. on it and spread it out on the roof. If any plane flies over the cabin, they'll see it and help us."

Randy frowned. "Don't you know how to spell 'Help'?"

Allie choked back a laugh. Nothing like a ten-year-old to add some chuckles when you needed them. Even Scott grinned as he explained that the letters S.O.S. meant the same thing as "Help."

"Come on, sport," Allie said as she playfully ruffled Randy's hair. "Let's look for something in the linen closet that will make a good sign. Right after supper, we'll paint it, and first thing in the morning we'll mount it on the roof. If the weather report is right, we're going to have our first clear day."

They ate an early supper of canned beans and creamed corn while it was still light and they didn't have to use the lantern. Scott was very frugal about burning any more oil than was necessary. They always put the children to bed early, and Scott and Allie brought in logs to keep a fire burning in the fireplace long after it was dark outside.

These quiet moments were some of Allie's favorite times. Sometimes they talked, sharing some personal happenings in their lives. Neither of them had been serious about anyone. But both of them had been on some humorous dates, usually blind dates set up by well-meaning friends, and they could laugh about them in retrospect. Reading by firelight was too much of a challenge, even though they both tried to pass the time with a couple of books from the bookcase. Most of the time they just enjoyed a companionable silence until the fire died down and they went to sleep.

They had about an hour of daylight left when they spread a dark green bedspread out on the living room floor, and Scott outlined a huge S.O.S. Both Randy and Cathy took turns filling in the bold letters with white paint until they got tired and were willing to let Allie and Scott help out. Allie had put a heavy blanket under the bedspread so the paint wouldn't go through and ruin the wide-planked floor.

"We'll have to add the blanket and bedspread to our IOU lists," she told Scott as they made their sign. "The list is getting longer and longer." She prayed that their absent hosts would someday know what a blessing their summer home had been.

When they'd finished and looked at their handiwork, there was a feeling of pride and accomplishment, almost as if they'd all contributed to a family project. "First thing tomorrow, we'll climb up and nail it on the roof," Scott said.

"Me, too? I climb around on roofs real good," Randy bragged.

"We'll see," Scott answered, knowing all the time that he wasn't about to let the boy up on a roof that was deeply slanted so snow would slip off of it. "Now it's time to get to bed."

He turned to Cathy, and laid his head on his folded hands as if they were a pillow. "Sleep," he said so she could read his lips.

The little girl smiled with her usual good humor. "It was fun painting," she said. "We made a big, big sign, didn't we?"

"You did a good job," Scott said as he swung Cathy up in his arms, and carried her into the bedroom. Allie and Randy followed.

When the two children were tucked in for the night, Scott left the room while Allie lingered to hear their childish prayers.

Her eyes were misty as she listened to Cathy's simple request, "Bless Mommy and Daddy and, God, bring me some new batteries."

Randy's muttered prayers were for his and God's ears alone, but Allie suspected he was asking the Almighty to make sure that he got the radio back.

She was smiling when she went back into the living room and closed the door. Then she sobered when she saw that Scott was about to go out the front door. "Where are you going?"

"Just out on the deck. Looks like the sky's clear and we might see a few stars."

"Wait a minute. I'll go with you."

"You'll probably need your jacket. You know how cool it gets at night."

"I'm fine," she said, moving quickly over to the door as he opened it. For some foolish reason, she didn't want him to leave her for even a few minutes outside. "I need some fresh air."

As they stepped out on the narrow deck, she drew in deep breaths of the brisk mountain air, clean and cool in the June night. A pungent smell of ponderosa pines and rich damp earth teased her nostrils and as she looked up at the heavens, never had an evening seemed so beautiful.

Scott leaned against the deck railing beside her. A deep indigo sky was like a velvet backdrop as moonlight touched the high ridge of Prospect Mountain. The rocky hillside was softened by dark shadows blending in thick stands of trees like the dark umber tones of an artist's brush.

"How peaceful everything is," she said softly, not wanting to disturb the stillness of the night. It was a moment for quiet contemplation, or tender murmurings.

She was surprised when Scott slipped his arm around her waist. His touch felt so natural, so familiar that she accepted it without thought. Their sudden closeness was so harmonious with the tranquility that surrounded them that neither spoke as they stood side by side, gazing up at the panorama of mountains, sky and stars. Their senses were filled with the beauty of the night, and blended with the magic of the night. There was something else, too—a dangerous awareness of each other.

She turned and looked at him. In the last few days she'd become aware of every line and plane in his face, and she knew that his every expression would be etched in her memory forever. He had made it clear that there was no future for any commitment they might make, and if she allowed herself to be caught up in the romance of the moment, there would be nothing ahead but pain for both of them.

"I think we'd better go in," she said as evenly as her quickened breathing would allow.

"Yes," he agreed quietly. As he looked into her face, Scott knew that if he tightened his embrace, she would lean into him, and never had he wanted to kiss her as much as he did at that moment. "Allie, you are so precious," he said with a catch in his throat. "I couldn't live with myself if I were the cause of your unhappiness. Do you understand what I'm saying?"

"I think so," she answered softly.

He leaned down and kissed her lightly, with no promise of anything deeper than a casual kiss between them. He couldn't live with himself if he hurt her by trying to live up to her deeply held expectations. He cared enough about her to warn her that there could never be a serious commitment between them. His voice was husky as he said, "Some lucky guy will be all that you want and more, Allie. Don't settle for anything less."

Allie pulled away without answering, turned and went into the house and left him standing on the deck alone. That night, she slept with her back to him, so he wouldn't see the glisten of tears on her cheeks.

Toward morning, Cathy cried out in a nightmare, and Scott went and got her before Allie could awaken. He brought the child into the living room to sleep with him on the rug. When Allie awoke and saw the two of them snuggled together, her heart was filled with both joy and sadness. She knew that last night on the deck they'd come to a turning in the road, and there was no going back. Scott's inherent nature was one of loving and caring. She was happy seeing him express this truth of his being, however reluctantly, but it was clear that Scott was intent upon denying that wonderful part of himself.

An early morning sun sent a blush of pink and apricot across the sky as if heralding the end of the devastating storm. A rainbow in the heavens wouldn't have been any more reassuring, and the Bible story had new meaning for Allie as she looked out the window and saw the earth bathed in sunshine.

They had a hurried breakfast, eating the last of the boxed cereal and powdered milk. She knew she'd have to be creative to put any kind of a meal on the table for lunch and supper. The pantry shelves were frightfully empty.

"All right, let's get at it," Scott said getting up from the table. He took a hammer and nails from the toolbox and with Allie's help, rolled up the bedspread.

Randy and Cathy scurried out the front door ahead of them. A redwood deck had been built across the front of the cabin, and all the reddish boards were saturated with rain. Scott could see that the asbestos shingles on the roof were dark with moisture, promising a slick footing. He'd never been fond of climbing around on high places, and he knew that this wasn't the time to take any kind of a tumble. He'd have to be extra careful and take plenty of time getting the cloth sign in place.

"What about a ladder?" Allie asked.

'I don't think we'll need one. See how low the roof overhang is? I should be able to stand on the deck railing, and pull myself up. Then you can hand things up to me."

Randy squinted up at the roof, then his eyes traveled to a vine trellis at one end of the deck. "Why don't ya climb up that way?"

"It won't hold me. No, Randy, don't even think about it," he ordered curtly when he saw the boy's purposeful frown. "You're not getting up on the roof. I can't be worrying about you sliding off."

Standing on the narrow deck railing was a balancing act in itself, and Allie watched Scott waver and then catch himself as he positioned his feet like a gymnast on a balancing beam. He leaned forward, grabbed one of the boards that ran along the edge of the roof behind a rain gutter and pulled himself upward.

She and the children stood a few feet away from the house and watched him move around the roof, nailing down the bedspread. He had just finished when a distant sound of a helicopter reached their ears.

Scott shouted from his perch on the roof and pointed, "There."

Allie's heart nearly stopped as she searched the skies. Where was it? Had they gotten their sign up just in time? She just had time to glimpse the helicopter as it disappeared on the other side of the mountain.

"Oh, no." Her heart sank. Scott was right. They were on the wrong side to be spotted by anyone searching the flooded canyon.

"Did they see our sign?" Randy asked with childish innocence.

"No, I'm afraid the helicopter was too far away."

"They'll be back," Scott said reassuringly when he'd gotten off the roof and joined them on the deck. "We just need to sit tight. We're plenty safe as long as we stay here."

The words were barely out when they heard an ominous rumble like a dozen bowling balls being rolled down the mountain behind the cabin. At first it was difficult to identify the location of the sound. The whole mountain seemed to be rumbling like a disgruntled beast.

"What the—" Scott's eyes flew upward to the high promontory and rock ledges at the crest of Prospect Mountain.

He saw in horror that rocks and earth were slipping downward, gathering momentum in a growing mudslide that threatened to cover everything in its path.

Chapter Thirteen

Mudslide!

They couldn't believe what they were seeing.

Before their eyes, a sliding mass of rocks, dirt and vegetation cut a wide swath in the mountainside as it moved downward from a high ridge to the valley below. The path of the slide grew wider and faster as the rolling mass gathered speed.

For a stunned moment, both Scott and Allie were mesmerized by the sudden horror of the scene. But the realization that the summer cabin could be leveled by the sliding mass jolted them into action.

"We have to get out of here!" Scott shouted. He turned around, picked up Cathy, and shouted, "Run!"

Allie grabbed Randy's hand, but with his usual stubbornness, he hung back. "I gotta get—"

"No, there isn't time! The mountain's coming down." She gestured with one hand as she pulled him down the deck steps with the other one. Then she shoved him ahead.

"Go. Run," she cried and sent him racing after Scott. She followed as fast as she could, struggling to maintain her own balance on the steeply slanted ground.

"This way," Scott shouted as they fled down the hillside, away from the cabin. There wasn't any time to go either right or left of the widening slide. He knew that their only hope was to get to the bottom of the hill, across a ravine and climb up the next hillside before the slide caught up with them.

"Hurry, hurry," he shouted over his shoulder as Cathy clung to his neck and buried her head in his shoulder. He would have preferred to carry her on his back, but there was no time to change positions. He knew that if his feet suddenly went out from under him in the slippery deadfall of needles and leaves, both of them would be thrown harshly to the ground and precious seconds would be lost.

Allie was thinking the same thing as she tried to keep her balance. The ground was soaked from the incessant rains and instantly changed to slippery mud as she stepped upon it.

As they fled through the trees, they could hear the rumbling earth coming closer and closer. A thick stand of aspen and pine trees lay between them and the ravine between the two wooded hillsides, and Scott prayed that the aspen would slow the slide long enough for them to get to the bottom of this hill and up the side of the next one.

Cathy clung to him the way she had in the rainstorm. Flinging an anxious look backward, Scott saw that Randy was making his own way down the hillside, a little distance to the right of Allie.

"Randy! Stay with us!" Scott shouted, afraid that the boy would get lost in the trees and lose them. No telling how difficult it would be to cross the ravine at the bottom and climb up the other side. "Stay with us!" he shouted again.

Either Randy didn't hear him or chose to ignore the order. In the next moment he was only a flash of color between the trees, and then disappeared altogether.

Stupid kid! Why would he strike out on his own after all they'd been through? Even if Randy made it safely down to the bottom of this hill, he could get lost trying to climb up the next wooded mountainside, fumed Scott. They sure didn't need that kind of complication. He kept glancing back to make sure Allie was coming behind him. He saw her slip once, but she righted herself and kept running.

As they broke out of the trees at the bottom of the hill, Scott was appalled to see that there was a flow of water in the ravine between the two mountains. A mountain steam?

How deep was it?

As he ran closer, he saw that it wasn't a regular riverbed, but just an overflow of rain from the runoff of the two mountainsides, but it was running swiftly. No telling what lay beneath the water. It could be dangerous footing trying to cross from one side to the other.

As Allie reached his side, he knew he had to make a decision and fast. If the trees didn't stop the mudslide it could sweep them into the water with the rest of the rocks, dirt and trees.

"Oh, dear Lord, what shall we do?" breathed Allie.

Scott knew that they had no choice but to ford the flowing water. "We have to cross!"

"Here! Here!" They heard Randy calling to them.

"Where are you?" Allie shouted back. They couldn't see him anywhere along the bank.

"Over here!"

"What the—" Scott's eyes widened when he saw Randy jumping up and down and waving from the other side of the building stream. Somehow the boy had crossed safely, and was standing on the opposite hillside.

"Come this way!" Randy shouted as he pointed to a place where the water was spilling over some submerged rocks. "This way! Come this way!"

They ran a few yards upstream and then both Scott and Allie blinked when they looked down at the place where Randy was pointing.

"Oh, no," Allie gasped as she viewed sprays of white water making liquid sculptures against boulders lying in a jagged line across the stream.

Scott certainly didn't like the looks of the rocks that would have made for precarious footing without the flow of water making them slippery, but there was no time to look for a safer place to cross. The swishing sound of flowing mud and the sharp crackle of breaking trees drove away all thoughts of delaying even a moment longer.

"Go," he ordered Allie.

She bit her lip and gingerly stepped out on the first boulder, and the next and the next.

Scott kept as close to her as he could as they felt their way through the water, cautiously putting their weight on each stepping stone. As before, Cathy's weight threatened to throw him dangerously off balance, but he managed to keep his footing as the water flowed around his legs and weighted his shoes.

Randy grinned like a cheerleader when they had safely reached the other side. "Good job," he said, mimicking a grown-up.

"Oh, Randy," Allie said his name thankfully, but there was no time for any more exchange.

"Climb," Scott ordered. He knew that once the slide reached the bottom of the hill, mud and debris would fill up the ravine. Just how far up it would reach on the mountainside where they sought safety was anybody's guess.

Glancing upward, he could see that there was a small plateau where the land leveled off about halfway to the mountain's craggy crest. This wide expanse of ground appeared to be flat and might even be a high mountain meadow, but he estimated it was more than an hour's climb to that high spot.

"Up. Up," he ordered. He knew they couldn't get there in one steady climb. In a short time all of them were breathing heavily, and their chests were burning in the high, oxygen-deprived air.

When Scott was sure they were high enough to avoid being overtaken by the encroaching mudslide, he stopped. "We'll rest here." He put down Cathy and smothered a groan as protesting back muscles caught in a spasm.

Allie dropped to the ground without a murmur. The first rush of adrenaline that had given her added energy had been used up, and the hard climb had demanded all her reserved strength. She doubted she could have broken into a run if all the forces of nature were at her back.

"You okay, Cathy?" Randy asked anxiously as he dropped down on the ground beside the little girl. When she didn't answer, he used his fingers to make an *O* and a *K*.

She nodded and then turned to look at Allie, her little anxious face filled with questioning. "What happened? Why did we run?"

No wonder the little girl was bewildered, thought Allie. She'd been snatched up and carried off without knowing the reason for the panic. The child hadn't heard the warning rumble that had sent them fleeing.

Before Allie could try and explain, Scott pointed toward the sloping hillside where moments before they had been fleeing for their lives. The slide was halfway down to the ravine, but it had taken a course that bypassed the cabin by a hundred yards or more. "Look at that! The slide missed the cabin!"

Allie couldn't believe her eyes. Nestled in a band of trees, they could see the roof of the cabin still intact.

Allie shouted in joy. Because of the configuration of the mountainside, the course of the mudslide had veered a safe distance to the eastern side of the cabin.

Scott felt his chest expand with relief. If there were

no more slides, it might be possible to make their way back to the cabin.

"It's a miracle," breathed Allie.

Scott smiled at Randy, and made a thumbs-up gesture that brought a wide grin to the boy's face. He winked at Cathy and her worried expression lessened. Even though the little girl didn't know what was making everyone happy, she was ready to join in.

Allie gave her a hug, kissed her cheek and mouthed, "Love you."

Showing that she understood, Cathy carefully used her hands and fingers to sign, "I love you."

The four of them sat together in an open area where rocks and low bushes gave them a view of the surrounding area. Gradually their breathing and heartbeats slowed to normal. Unlike their former flight in the rain, they were dry except for shoes and stockings, which had been soaked crossing the stream of water. A blessed sun in a clear sky bathed them in warmth and light, and only a few wispy clouds like white lace trailed across barren peaks that formed the Continental Divide.

After their terrifying flight, the moment of blessed safety was almost unreal. Scott sat cross-legged on the ground, watching the opposite hillside like a sentinel assigned to catch the first warning signs of another rockslide.

Allie had the children sitting on each side of her. She tried to answer Randy's questions about why the mountain was falling down, and his childish demands about what they were going to do next.

"We'll have to wait and see," she said vaguely,

not having the least idea how they were going to cope with this new situation. Only the blessed change in the weather made their plight any different from their former predicaments. They were without food, shelter and once again at the mercy of the elements.

Scott wasn't ready to share his thoughts and growing concerns. He knew that the unrelenting rain had saturated the earth, loosening rocks from their moorings and turning mountain soil into slippery mud. Even the movement of a small dislodged boulder could have been the trigger for the mudslide, and like a snowball rolling down a winter hill, the moving mass of rocks and dirt had expanded to frightening proportions.

When Scott got to his feet and walked over to a mound of granite boulders and climbed up on them to see better, Allie told the children to stay put, and she followed him.

"Do you think there'll be another one?" Allie asked, as if reading his thoughts. She could tell that he was tensely searching the mountain for any sign of movement.

"I don't know," he answered honestly. What worried Scott was the possibility that other loosened boulders on the high ridge would momentarily start another treacherous flow down the same hillside. He kept his eyes glued to the high shelf of rocks where the first slide had begun. "Maybe everything that's loose has already come down."

"Then it would be safe to return to the cabin?" she asked, hopefully.

"Maybe. If no more come down today, it's unlikely that there'll be any more loosened rock until the next heavy rain.'' He searched the western horizon for any sign of clouds that might be the harbinger of another storm. Only some wispy white clouds trailed over the high granite peaks like the froth of a wedding veil.

"The radio said that the weather was going to be clear for the next few days,'' she reminded him.

Then suddenly he stiffened and she couldn't tell why he had suddenly gone as rigid as a gatepost. "What is it?''

Randy was jumping up and shouting, ''Look! Look!''

Then she saw a speck in the sky growing larger and larger as a helicopter came into view, flying over the high ridge where the mudslide had begun.

Both Allie and Scott held their collective breaths as they watched the copter begin to circle around over Prospect Mountain. Would it come low enough to see the cabin? Would it spy their sign on the roof? At first it seemed that the helicopter would be too far south to get a good look at the northern side of the mountain, and then, almost imperceptibly, the helicopter made an exaggerated turn and came back.

"They saw it!'' shouted Scott. ''They're flying over the cabin!''

"Yahoo!'' yelled Randy, clapping his hands, and doing an Indian dance.

Cathy started copying Randy's antics, jumping up and down and clapping her hands, too.

Scott grabbed Allie and gave her a bear hug that fairly squeezed the breath out of her. She laughed with him as they watched the helicopter hovering high above the cabin for a long moment before it turned and disappeared once more over the top of the mountain.

Scott grinned from ear to ear. "They'll report it to a ground rescue crew, and I'm betting it won't be very long before someone shows up at our doorstep driving a vehicle that will take us out of here."

"Does that mean we have to walk all the way back?" Randy asked, his exuberance quickly disappearing.

"Unless you sprout wings in the next few minutes, I—" Scott broke off in mid-sentence, spun around and shielded his eyes with his hand.

A warning rumble increased to thundering proportions as another large chunk of the high rocky ledge broke away and began tumbling down the hillside above the cabin.

"No, no," Allie cried as they watched the new slide create its own destructive path. As before, the cabin was miraculously spared as a large swath of earth, rocks and vegetation were swept downward. In less than two minutes, the mudslide had reached the bottom of the ravine, spilling more debris into the narrow fault between the hills.

Allie and Scott stood motionless until the last stream of mud and rocks had hit the bottom. Neither of them could put into words what they felt. Twice the cabin had been spared, but what were the chances of a third slide?

From their position on the mountainside, they could look down into the ravine where the two mudslides had flowed down into the flowing water between the mountains.

"It's damning up the water," Scott cried, as the ravine filled up with rocks, splintered trees and tons of wet earth.

Allie saw in horror that water that had been flowing through the cut in the mountain before the mudslides was now backing up and filling the whole area below them with water. As far as they could see was nothing but deep water as the mudslides formed a natural dam.

The decision about whether or not they should return to the cabin was one that they never had to make. There was no way to cross the growing body of water that was forming a narrow lake between the two mountains.

Randy and Cathy were still laughing and jumping around in glee, but Allie and Scott looked at each other in stunned silence. Roller-coaster emotions of the last few minutes had swept them up into high jubilation only to drop them down into sickening depths of disbelief and disappointment.

The summer cabin had been spared. Everything within its warm walls was still there. They could glimpse it through the trees, but it would be easier to hike miles over the rugged mountain terrain to find other shelter than to try and return to the comforts they had known there.

As if the truth could be denied, Allie refused to accept what her eyes were seeing. "There has to be a way across the ravine, Scott," she argued.

"I don't see how," he answered grimly.

"But both mudslides missed the cabin. All we have to do is wait and make sure that no more rock ledges above it have been dislodged. Once the danger is past we can return to the cabin and wait for someone to come."

"Allie, the whole ravine is filled with mud and water in both directions, and we're trapped on this side of it. No telling how many miles the flow of the slide has gone, filling up the cut between these mountains. It could go on for miles, and the water is getting higher all the time. There's no way to get back to the other side of the ravine."

"But, if we stay here—" Her voice broke, and suddenly all the reserve strength that she'd been drawing upon deserted her. She covered her face with her hands as a swell of hot tears spilled into her eyes.

"Don't, Allie, don't," he pleaded, quickly reaching out to her. He was unprepared for her sudden collapse.

She tried to turn away so that he and the children couldn't see her crying, but suddenly he had his arms around her, drawing her close, and stroking her head as if she were a child. His tenderness just made her emotional collapse even worse. Choked sobs caught in her throat.

"It's all right. It's all right," he soothed. "Just don't give out on me now."

"I'm sorry, I'm sorry."

He felt her trembling as she struggled to regain control. Until that moment, he hadn't realized how much he'd depended upon her courage and strong faith. In spite of everything that had happened to them, she'd been his support. She'd helped him draw on an inner strength that he didn't know he had. If the truth were known, he'd been scared that he wouldn't be able to come through for her and the kids. In the last few years he had made sure that no one depended upon him for anything, and by the same token, he had been determined not to be dependent on anybody but himself.

As she trembled in his arms, a protective urge he would have denied before the flood made his voice husky. "Honey, it's going to be all right. We're not licked yet."

She recognized his attempt to lighten the new challenges that faced them. They had fled the cabin without anything but the jackets and clothes they were wearing. No supplies, blankets or food. Now they were stranded on a hillside with no way to go back and get anything they might need. Her prayers of thanksgiving suddenly seemed a mockery to the disintegrating situation in which they found themselves.

"Allie...Allie," Scott murmured her name and tightened his arms around her.

She lay her head against his chest, knowing that she had to pull herself together. Physically she felt as if someone had been beating on her, and emotionally her nerves were shredded. Facing a mountain of new challenges was more than her exhausted mind and spirit could handle at the moment. Closing her eyes, she drew on the warmth of his body, the steadiness of his embrace.

"Are you okay now?" he asked.

She nodded, and was startled when he pulled away, and held her at arm's length.

Looking straight into her eyes, he said firmly, "This is no time for you to lose that stubborn pride of yours, Allie. Sure, we've had a couple of setbacks, but I don't know what we could have done differently. How did we know the cabin would be spared? And there wasn't any time to prepare for what has happened. Whether we like it or not, we've got to cope the best we can. And I need your help. The kids need your help. Understand?"

"I'm sorry. I'm just so…discouraged. I can't bear to think of us spending a cold night on this mountain with two frightened, hungry children."

"What about all that stuff you were giving me about the Lord providing? Don't tell me you've decided to throw in the towel where all that faith business is concerned."

"No, of course not." Her chin came up. *Even though He slay me, still will I trust Him.*

"Well, you could have fooled me. If I ever saw anyone ready to desert the ranks of believers, it's you." When he saw a fiery glint replace the dull, flat glaze in her eyes, he knew his taunting had done its work.

"Don't think I don't know what you're doing," she countered with more energy than she knew she had. As she wiped away her tears, she admitted, "I guess I deserved a little mental spanking. Thank you."

He gave her a wry grin. "Any time."

"All right, what's next?"

"I'm not sure," he admitted, relieved that she'd

recovered herself and was showing her usual self-composure. "We really don't have that many choices, but I don't see the advantage of staying where we are."

Randy and Cathy had been watching them with wide, anxious eyes, so Allie walked over to them, dropped down on the ground beside them and said, "Everything's going to be fine."

"Then why are you bawling?" Randy asked with his usual bluntness.

"Because I thought we could go back to the cabin and have everything we enjoyed while we were there," she said honestly. "But we can't."

"Why can't we?" Randy demanded.

Allie explained that the water was no longer just a stream but a deep lake that wouldn't allow them to go back across the ravine. "So we have to make the best of things."

"What are we going to eat?"

"I don't know."

"Where are we going to sleep?"

"I don't know."

"That's enough, Randy," Scott cut in abruptly. The boy wasn't the only one asking questions, and Scott didn't have any of the answers.

The midday sun was straight overhead, so there was time to find shelter for the night, if any existed within hiking distance, but they weren't high enough to see much of the surrounding terrain. One thing was clear, they couldn't go down, and trying to move sideways on the mountain wouldn't improve the situation. The flooded ravine would still keep them from getting anywhere close to the cabin. What good would the roof sign do now?

As if Allie was tracking his thoughts, she said, "Even if the helicopter reported our S.O.S., I don't see how a rescue team would get to the cabin now."

"The road's gone, that's for sure," he admitted. "And there's no place to land a helicopter on the side of the dammed-up ravine. No telling how long it would be before someone could get in and out of the place."

"At least we'd have food and shelter while we waited if only we'd stayed in the cabin," she lamented.

"True enough, but the choice wasn't ours. There was no way to know that we would have been safe if we hadn't run. Hindsight is always twenty-twenty." He cleared his throat. "Okay, troops. On your feet. We've got a little climbing to do. Look on the bright side. The sun is shining and it's not raining."

The pep talk did little to brighten their faces. He motioned for Cathy to get on his back, but she shook her head and let him know that she wanted to do her own climbing.

"All right, honey." He nodded to show her that he understood. She was a remarkable little girl, trusting, adaptable and basically happy in spite of the challenges that her lack of hearing presented. He promised himself to do everything in his power to get her safely back to her parents. He'd keep his eye on her and when she began to get tired, he'd put her on his back again.

"Where we going?" Randy asked as if they were

following some kind of a map, and Scott had a destination already marked out.

"Up," he said simply because that answer was the only one he could give. At the moment he didn't know if they'd be climbing in a straight line, or zigzagging around rock outcroppings and heavy vegetation that barred their way.

As before when they were climbing, Scott took the lead with the two children between him and Allie. As they struggled upward, he kept his eye on the small plateau where the mountain leveled off. If they could camp out on flat ground it would be a blessing, reasoned Scott, and the chances of someone seeing them from the air would be better than on the wooded, sloping hills.

Allie kept hoping that another helicopter might fly over the area. There was no way for the copter to know that the help sign on the cabin was obsolete. Any rescuers that made their way there would only find an empty cabin.

The saturated ground was a challenge, but the southern side of this mountain had more trees and vegetation to hold the earth in place, and there were no rock ledges above to increase the worry of a mudslide.

They stopped three times to rest and each time, Cathy shook her head when Scott offered to carry her. At one of the rest breaks, Randy turned furtively and drew something from his jacket pocket, handed it to Cathy and then glared at Scott and Allie as if expecting them to light into him for hiding something from them.

Scott raised a questioning eyebrow at Allie. What had the boy squirreled away? She shrugged and waited to see what Cathy was going to do with the small packet in her hands. What was it? Very carefully the little girl broke open the cellophane wrapping.

Graham crackers. Allie smothered a smile. Randy must have lifted them from the pantry and hidden them in his jacket.

Without hesitation Cathy offered one to Allie and Scott and Randy. "Have a cracker." Then she bit into the last one herself, her eyes bright and innocent. How trusting and adaptable Cathy was, thought Allie, as if her handicap had taught her to take each moment as it came.

"Good thinking, Randy," Scott said, nodding in appreciation. "You were smart to put these in your pocket in case we might have needed them. I wish I'd done the same thing."

Allie noticed that neither she nor Scott was eating the crackers. They were saving them for the children. No telling how long it would be before the next bit of food came their way.

"I'm thirsty," Randy said when he'd finished his cracker and looked at Scott.

Water! thought Scott. The key to survival.

The sun was quickly burning off all the rain that had collected in any cup-like indentations in the rocks. Even trying to lick up the moisture like an animal would not provide the water they needed to keep alive. Their only hope was to find a spring or a runoff of water from the high country. At the moment, though, finding some rainwater was the best bet.

"Let's have a look in those rocks," he told Randy, "and see if we can find a natural bowl that might have some rain left in it."

While he and the two children hiked over to some layered rocks, Allie leaned back against a boulder and closed her eyes. All of her life, a morning meditation ritual was like a spiritual vitamin taken daily to strengthen her for challenges in her work and personal life. Never had she needed a spiritual pick-me-up more than she did at that moment. *Our Father, who art in heaven...*

When Scott and the kids returned from their unsuccessful hunt for rainwater, he saw that tired lines had eased in Allie's face and a visible glow of serenity touched her lovely features. All evidence of tearful anxiety was gone. His heart softened as he looked at her, and in a way he felt sorry for her because he knew that she still clung to a trust and faith that had little relevancy to real life. He didn't believe for one minute "all things work to the good of those who love the Lord," and he wasn't about to depend upon some magnanimous God to get them safely off this mountain.

"Ready?" he asked after a few minutes.

Allie smiled. "Ready."

Cathy was tired enough to let Scott carry her the rest of the way, and when they reached the flat promontory he had spied from below, he gladly set her down.

"We made it," Allie gasped. The last hundred

yards had been grueling, and they all were breathing heavily in the high, thin air, trying to get enough oxygen into their lungs to feed their weary muscles. She sat down on the ground and looked around in awe of the tiny mountain meadow with its tasseled wild green grass, red patches of Indian paintbrush flowers and lovely blue and white columbines. Patches of scrub oak, low junipers and ragged cedar bushes dotted the flat landscape, cupped by jagged rock cliffs rising dramatically to a high pinnacle.

The view from this high mountain perch was spectacular, with a vista of sky and high mountains surrounding them. Scott realized with a sickening plunge of his stomach that this flat cleft of the mountain might not have been the wisest choice for their survival. There was no way they could climb higher even if they'd been seasoned mountain climbers. The terrain was too rugged to explore the rock cliffs for water and, unless there was a hidden spring seeping downward through rock layers edging the flat land, they would have to retreat down the hill again in hopes of finding life-giving water.

Allie wished she had Randy's and Cathy's resiliency as they began to explore, excitedly picking up pieces of petrified wood that had been a living tree countless years before.

"Do you think there might be some Indian arrowheads?" Randy asked excitedly. Lily had brought some for show, and had encouraged the children to keep their eyes open for them on their hikes.

"Maybe," she said even though she doubted very much that this high, isolated meadow could have been hunting grounds. As they bounded about, she warned them, "Stay away from the edge of the cliff." The earth fell away in a spectacular drop and only hardy, sturdy scrub oaks clung to the steep incline below.

She could tell that Scott was worried. She couldn't bear to think that they would have to retrace their steps down the treacherous hillside, but she knew they would have no choice if they didn't find water.

Scott squinted against an afternoon sun that was beginning its descent behind the high mountain peaks. "I think we'd better see what kind of protection those rocks will give us for the night," he told Allie.

She nodded. "Come on, kids," she called and motioned to Randy and Cathy.

Neither of them paid her any attention. They were intent on watching something overhead. Allie looked upward and saw two beautiful bald eagles circling the high cliffs. The spread of their wings was magnificent and their glides were smooth and graceful. It was almost as if they were putting on an aerial demonstration as they rose and fell, dipped and soared, and circled overhead.

"They must have a nest in those high rocks," Scott said.

"Beautiful," Allie murmured, totally captivated by the beauty of their flight.

Cathy clapped her hands, looking upward, and unwittingly backing up precariously near the edge of the cliff. For a moment no one noticed her, and then Allie's heart leaped into her throat as the little girl took another step backward.

"No, Cathy no!" Allie cried, leaping to her feet,

but her warning never reached the child's deaf ears. Darting forward, she reached Cathy just as the little girl turned and ran toward Randy who had caught her eye and was motioning her to come to him.

A moment of thankfulness was lost as the earth beneath Allie's feet began to crumble before she was able to move away from the edge. The weight of her body was too much for the rain-weakened shelf, and with a rumbling sound, the ledge gave way as the ground dropped out from under her.

Allie screamed.

She tried to grab anything that would stop her fall but her hands only flailed empty air. In a cascade of rocks and dirt, she was carried down the rugged slope until she was plunged into a thicket of scrub oak bushes that miraculously stopped her downward slide. Pelted by fallen rock and choked by dirt, she tried to get up before the small bushes gave way under her weight.

She had made it to her knees before a football-size boulder came flying down from above. With a shattering sound, it struck her head. She cried out as burning pain radiated through her skull like an onslaught of hot pokers.

"Allie, Allie." She heard her name being called through layers of a dark haze. Then her body went limp and she slipped away into unconsciousness.

Chapter Fourteen

"Allie! Allie!" he screamed in panic. *No! No!*

Horror ran through Scott's veins like searing fire as he bolted toward Allie. He'd been a short distance away checking some rocks for a possible hidden spring when he'd heard her piercing cry. Swinging around, what he saw in a flash sent his heart thumping like the roar of surf in his head. One second she was standing on the edge of the cliff but even before he could reach her, she had dropped out of sight.

He raced to the edge of the cliff and, looking downward, he saw her body tumbling over and over, pelted by rock and sliding dirt. Then it happened! One second she was sliding downward, and the next instant, her fall was stopped! By some chance beyond belief, a drift of oak bushes had stopped her plunge about fifty feet below.

Both children ran crying over to Scott, trying to see what had happened. "Where's Allie? Where's Allie?"

"Stay back! Stay back!" He shoved them away from the edge. "I'm going after her."

Quickly, he let himself down over the edge, which was less sharp since part of the earth had fallen away with Allie's fall. Scrambling to keep his footing on the rocky incline, he sent dirt and pebbles sliding down the hillside ahead of him. Skidding, slipping, half-running he made his way down to where she was snarled in the thickly wooded shrubs.

When he reached her, his heart sank. She was lying still in a crumpled heap. Her eyes were closed.

"Allie, darling. Allie," he cried, but she didn't respond to his voice.

As he bent over her, he saw that she was bleeding from a wound at the side of her head. She'd been struck by one of the jagged rocks and knocked unconscious, he reasoned. Her arms and legs seemed to be in a normal position, and there was no outward sign of broken bones.

I can't leave her here.

As he looked below, a sickening bile rose in his throat. Nothing would stop a downward plunge for hundreds of feet. Any moment their weight could dislodge the roots of the bushes and pull them from the ground. He was afraid that even the slightest movement pulling her free might break the mesh of branches holding her, and then they both would be pounded to death by the rocky fall.

He had no choice. He had to try and carry her back up the slope. With strength drawn from some miraculous well, he lifted her slender body up in his arms. His muscular body had been conditioned to climbing while carrying Cathy so much of the way. With laborious step after step, he carried her back up the slope. Both of them were covered with her blood when he laid her on flat ground a safe distance from the place where the edge had crumbled under her weight.

Cathy was crying hysterically, wailing, "Allie... Allie."

Randy's rounded eyes matched his white face and trembling lips. "Is she all right? Is she all right?"

Scott tore his shirt into strips and then wadded the cloth against her head wound and tied it into a clumsy bandage to hold pressure on the bleeding.

He felt her pulse and roughly estimated over a hundred heartbeats per minute. Her breathing was irregular and labored. At that moment, he knew that all his efforts would not be enough.

An afternoon sun was already lowering toward the ridge of high western peaks. In a few hours, purple twilight would spread across the valley, and then it would be night. Dark and cold. Stranded on this mountainside without medical help, she would die.

Seeing the despair in his face, Randy croaked, "What are you gonna do?"

"There's nothing I can do...*except pray.*"

The words came to his lips from deep within the recesses of his being, like a planted seed waiting to be brought into fruition. Surrender brought tears into his eyes as he bowed his head over Allie's unconscious body. He admitted that he had been denying God's presence in his life, but at this moment, he knew that there was no other power that could save Allie's life except some almighty presence.

As he bowed his head, both the children took his hands, and together they prayed for help. Words did not come easily for him. Since Jimmy's death, he'd been building a void between himself and the Divine. He remembered Allie's strong trust that God would protect them, and he drew on her firm faith now as he prayed, *I believe. Help Thou my unbelief.*

Cradling Allie's head in his lap, he sat with slumped shoulders, listening to her labored breathing and watching the red, soaked patch of lovely golden hair grow larger and larger. His clumsy efforts to stop the bleeding had failed. She looked so fragile, so vulnerable that his heart constricted with a growing love as he stroked her cheek. *It's my fault. I should have been paying more attention to her and the kids.*

He'd made the mistake of thinking that there was no danger to them once they'd reached the high plateau. The mountain meadow was peaceful enough, and watching the eagles had taken the children's minds off their dire situation. Now he realized that he should have warned Cathy and Randy to stay away from the edge, but he hadn't.

Cathy snuggled close to him, quietly sobbing, "Allie, Allie, what's the matter with Allie?" Randy couldn't sit still. The boy was up and down, anxiously waiting for something to happen.

"Don't you go near that edge," Scott warned as the two eagles appeared again and Randy watched them soar and dive almost overhead.

They must be looking for prey in the wild grass,

thought Scott. Maybe they had young ones to feed. The thought made Scott realize that he had to find some kind of food and water for survival of the two young ones in his care.

Allie would want him to take care of the children at all cost. At all cost. *No, Allie, no.* The words were too ominous. If she died in his arms like this, how could he live with himself?

He'd never felt such total despair as he did at that moment, and when Randy started shouting and waving toward the eagle's nest, he opened his mouth to lash out at him.

The angry words died in his throat.

"Look! Look!" Randy cried, pointing to the sky.

It wasn't another eagle that was flying over the high ridge, realized Scott. The growing, large black spot could only be one thing—a helicopter circling the area.

In an instant Scott had eased Allie's head from his lap and was on his feet. *Please, God, let them see us.* He grabbed up his torn shirt, waved it like a flag.

He shouted at Randy, "Run around in a circle. Dance. Wave your arms. Do something to catch their attention!"

Even though they knew that the sound would never reach the whirlybird, the two of them screamed and waved frantically. Cathy stayed by Allie's side, her eyes wide with wonder as she watched the helicopter and the circling eagles.

At first it seemed that the aircraft would miss the plateau and continue toward the hill where the mudslides had taken place, but almost imperceptibly, the helicopter changed course and turned in their direction.

The two eagles continued to float and circle above the mountain meadow as if marking the spot where the aircraft could land on the flat ground. As the helicopter came closer, the huge birds disappeared back into the high cleft of the mountain.

Scott knew that the pilot had seen them when it hovered for a long moment above them, kicking up blinding dirt. The copter blades cut the air with a whipping buzz before it very slowly set down a short distance away on the flat area.

Flying dust mingled with tears flowing down Scott's check as he breathed a prayer of thanksgiving. Randy started yelling and doing one of the Indian dances that he'd learned. Then he pulled Cathy to her feet and signed the word, "home." Her tear-stained little face glowed with sudden joy, and she hugged him as if he were the one who had brought the plane to fly them home.

Two attendants and the pilot jumped out of the copter the minute the blades stopped whirling. Scott ran to meet them.

"Any injuries?" asked the female flight nurse, immediately spying Allie's prone figure on the ground some distance away.

"Yes, hurry."

"What happened?" asked the husky male paramedic as they hurried over to Allie's side.

"She fell. Hit her head. A concussion, I think," Scott told them in jerky sentences. "I tried to stop the bleeding."

After one quick look at Allie's head, they immediately brought a stretcher and their black equipment bags. Kneeling beside Allie's prone figure, they hurriedly began to check her vital signs.

"Has she been unconscious since the fall?" the nurse asked.

Scott nodded. "I got to her in less than a couple of minutes. She was out when I reached her."

"How long ago was that?"

An eternity.

He ran an agitated hand through his hair. Time had stopped from the second he saw Allie drop out of view. "Less than an hour, I think. I carried her back up here." Then he added quickly, "I knew it was dangerous to move her, but I had no choice. Any moment she could have tumbled farther down the hillside. I couldn't chance it. I had to move her." He took a deep breath to try and settle his shaky voice. "I couldn't leave her there." The way a falling body would be battered and beaten in such a disastrous fall brought a cold prickling to his skin.

"Sometimes moving a victim is the lesser of two evils," the nurse replied evenly as she lifted each of Allie's eyelids and flashed a small penlight into her eyes.

"Equal and reactive," she said to her companion, and then quickly put an oxygen mask over Allie's face.

"Blood pressure, 90/60. Pulse, 100. I'll start an IV," he said as he pulled tubes and needles from the open bag.

The nurse checked for broken bones, and found

none, but she said, "We'd better put her on a board before we move her. There may be some internal injuries."

Randy and Cathy had been watching with rounded eyes, and the pilot, a friendly young fellow started talking to them in a reassuring way. "How are you kids doing?" He eyed their disheveled look, and smiled at Cathy.

"She can't hear," Randy told him when the pilot tried to put Cathy at ease by telling her that everything was going to be okay.

The pilot looked around vaulting cliffs and the deep canyon that lay below, walked over to Scott and asked bluntly, "How in blazes did you get way up here?"

"We hiked."

"From where?" The man looked puzzled. "The flood was on the southern side of the Prospect Mountain. We didn't expect anyone would climb this far to get away from the water."

Scott explained what had transpired after the camp had flooded.

"Well, you're lucky some eagles caught our attention and we looked in this direction. Are you okay?" he asked, looking at Randy.

It was obvious that Cathy had been crying, so Scott assured him quickly. "The kids are tired and hungry, but they're fine."

Randy kept staring at the pair of silver wings pinned to the pilot's uniform. His fascination was so obvious that the pilot smiled and said, "I bet you two kids would like to see inside my copter, wouldn't you? And how about I take you both for a nice ride in a few minutes?''

Randy nodded eagerly and grabbed Cathy's hand. The pilot walked them over to the waiting copter. Scott hung back staying close to Allie as the two medics carefully transferred her from the ground onto the stretcher. With practiced ease, they picked it up and moved quickly toward the copter's open door.

While they concentrated on their patient, the pilot directed Scott and the children to seats near the cockpit. With the ease of an elevator rising in mid-air, the copter lifted off, and moments later they were whirling away in an easterly direction.

Randy had his nose pressed against the window, and was reluctant to take time to drink the hot broth they were given. Cathy curled up against Scott. Her eyelids drooped as weariness overtook her, and she fell asleep.

Using his radio, the pilot alerted rescue headquarters that they were on their way to Denver's Saint Joseph's Hospital with four survivors of the flood. Scott gave him the names of Cathy and Randy, and asked him to pass along reassurance to the parents that the children were safe and well.

''Allie's parents are dead,'' he told the pilot when he asked about Allie's family. He gave him Trudy's name because she was the only friend Scott knew who was close to Allie. There were probably other people who should be notified about the accident but he realized with painful regret that he knew very little about her personal life.

Scott slumped in his seat, and as he watched the

medics hover over Allie's motionless body, he mourned the wasted moments with her that he'd let slip by. She had pushed her way back into his life, and he had resented it. If the flood hadn't happened, he would have readily turned his back on her. *I'm sorry, Allie. I'm sorry I was so pig-headed.*

He remembered how distant he had been when she first came to ask him to let them have their church camp. He'd deliberately tried to keep his distance from her at the camp. Every time he'd begun to feel at all close to her, he'd shut down his feelings. After they'd been thrown together, forced to put everything aside and concentrate on survival, all his defenses against her had begun to crumble. He'd discovered that she was still the same wonderful, precious person and, almost too late, he'd wished that they hadn't let time and distance separate them. She no longer felt the same way about him, and he could understand why. Now, all he wanted was for her to recover and find the perfect soul mate her heart desired.

As the copter set down on the roof of the hospital, a medical team met them with a gurney and, very efficiently, they removed Allie through the open door of the helicopter. In less than a minute, they had swiftly disappeared with Allie into the E.R.

Scott and the children headed into the waiting room, a cry of relief greeting them as Mike and Peggy Crawford ran with open arms to embrace their daughter. Hugging and kissing her, they kept saying, "Thank God. Thank God."

As Scott and Randy stood and watched, Scott kept

his hand on the boy's shoulder. Where were Randy's foster parents?

"Bless you. Bless you," Peggy Crawford kept saying to Scott. "We kept praying that somehow our little girl would be found safe."

He handled their praise as best he could, but his mind was on Allie and he wanted to get away from them as quickly as he could.

"The church kept a nightly vigil for both Allie and the two missing children," Mike Crawford told him. "We've been praying for those who have lost their lives and for those who are still unaccounted for. I guess the good Lord added your name to our prayers," he said sincerely, and touched Scott on the shoulder. "A real Rocky Mountain miracle."

Cathy grabbed Randy's hand, pulled him forward, and said, "This is my friend, Randy. He was good to me," she said simply. As her mother and father hugged Randy and thanked him, Cathy smiled broadly.

"Will you take Randy home with you until his foster parents can pick him up?" Scott asked. "I've got to stay here at the hospital."

"Sure. Our pleasure. Is that all right with you, Randy?" Cathy's mother asked, and the boy's smile was answer enough.

Mike Crawford asked, "What happened to Allie?"

Scott replied briefly that she'd fallen. He didn't want the Crawfords to know that their daughter had been the cause of the accident.

"Is there anything we can do that would help her?" Mike asked.

"Just pray," he heard himself saying. If anyone deserved their prayers it was Allie. Scott hurriedly left them and began the tortuous vigil of waiting, waiting.

After he'd made a call to his mother and assured her that he was all right, he pestered everyone he could to get information on Allie's condition, and one sympathetic nurse tried to keep him informed.

"The doctor is examining her."

"They've taken her to X-ray for a CAT scan."

"She's being moved from E.R. to I.C.U."

"They may let you see her when she's settled in."

Scott waited outside the intensive care unit for more than two hours before he was allowed to see her for five minutes.

"Allie, Allie," he whispered in a hoarse voice as he looked down at her prone figure. Her face was waxy-white, and her hands lay lifeless at her side. As he stood beside her bed, he was grateful for all the machines, tubes and monitors connected to her lithe body, and at the same time, repelled by the sight.

Keep fighting, Allie. Don't give up.

He'd never known a more vivacious, independent, strong spirit than Allie's, and to see her so vulnerable and weak shook him to the depths of his being. He would have given his own life to spare hers and he'd never forgive himself for not taking better care of her.

A gray-haired doctor spoke to Scott after his five-minute visit was over. "I understand you're one of the survivors of the flood." He glanced at Scott's blood-splattered grimy clothes, and then smiled. "I guess there's no question about that. I hear that you rescued the patient after a fall, and probably saved her life, as well.''

"How is she?'

"Well, she bled heavily, but by stanching the blood flow, you kept her from bleeding to death.''

"Then she's going to be all right?''

He frowned. "We've given her several pints of blood, and her vital signs are good. She has a severe concussion, and is in a deep coma. The prognosis is guarded. We're keeping her sedated until the swelling goes down. Then we'll know more.''

On that sober note, the doctor returned to the I.C.U. with its incessant hum of monitoring machines, and Scott dropped down on one of the sofas in the waiting room.

One motherly nurse tried to get him to find some place to clean up and rest, but Scott refused to leave the hospital. Totally exhausted mentally, emotionally and physically, he buried his face in his hands. A few minutes later when he felt a hand on his shoulders, he slowly raised his head.

"Scott, oh my God,'' Trudy breathed when she saw his drawn face, lifeless eyes and the droop of his slack mouth. "Is she— Has she—'' Died?

He shook his head. "Allie's in a coma.''

Trudy sat down beside him. "What do the doctors say?''

"Not much.'' Scott repeated what he knew. "All we can do is wait.''

"I came as quickly as I could. I still can't believe it. When I got the call from a rescue unit, I had them repeat the message three times to make sure I wasn't dreaming." Tears flowed down her plump cheeks. "I've been beside myself. Living the horrible nightmare over and over again, thinking if only I'd done this, if only I'd done that—"

"It doesn't do any good to try and reshape the past," he said as much to himself as to her.

"Where have you been all this time?"

Her eyes grew wide and her mouth dropped open in surprise when he told her about their stay in the summer cabin.

"You mean that you and Allie were holed up all cozy-like in a mountain cabin for three days? Well, I'll be." Her misty eyes sparkled. "I guess you got to know each other pretty good. I mean, shut off from the rest of the world like that. Who would have thought it?"

Scott knew full well that Trudy was curious to know if anything romantic occurred between them. "I'll confess that those few days are some of the happiest I've ever known." *And I was a fool not to realize it.*

When Trudy asked him why they just didn't stay safe and sound in the cabin until someone came along to rescue them, he explained about the mudslides. Her expression sobered when he described Allie's fall and their rescue by the helicopter.

Watching his face, she said quietly, "I'd say that was something of a miracle, wouldn't you?"

Drawing a deep breath, he said, "And now we need another one."

"Well, Allie always told me that she liked to keep prayed-up, so she didn't have to depend on any 911 spiritual calls to get her out of trouble.'' Trudy signed. ''We just have to make sure our faith is just as strong.''

They sat in silence until the hour was up, and it was time for another five-minute visit.

''They usually only let family go in,'' Scott told Trudy.

''Then I'll be her sister.''

The next few days showed little improvement in Allie's condition. She remained in a coma, her breathing continued to be strong and her body reflexes to pain were encouraging as they tested the balls of her feet and squeezed the knuckles in her hand.

Scott and Trudy were at the hospital every day, and sometimes late into the night. When Allie's condition stabilized, she was moved to a private room. They took turns staying with her.

Scott rented a motel room near the hospital, bought some new clothes and became a daily fixture at the hospital. He didn't know what to do but fill her room with flowers. He couldn't stay away from the hospital, even going back in the middle of a sleepless night. The staff got used to seeing the handsome, dark-haired man walking the halls at night, or standing with slumped shoulders as he stared out a darkened window.

He had taken to talking to her, the way they had done in front of the fireplace, sharing some memories of his summers with his dad that he'd forgotten. As it turned out, he was with her when she showed the first signs of regaining consciousness.

Allie heard his voice as a faint echo. In that boundless state of nothingness, she wanted to bring the voice closer, but even as she tried, it faded away and was lost. The next time the enveloping haze began to part, his voice grew louder and more distinct.

At first, Scott thought he was just imagining the first flicker of her eyelids, but a shot of hope brought him out of the chair beside her bed. "Allie, Allie. Honey, can you hear me?"

There was no doubt about it. Her eyelids flickered even though they seemed too heavy for her to lift.

Scott rang the bell for the nurse. "She was coming out of it. I know she was. I saw her eyelids flutter."

The nurse watched and waited.

Nothing happened.

Another day passed and when the doctor made his rounds and went through the usual routine of testing her for touch and sound, he was rewarded with a noticeable response. Very slowly Allie began to return to consciousness.

The first time she fully opened her eyes, she saw a blurred face bending over her.

"If you hear me, squeeze my hand," the doctor ordered.

She couldn't tell whether she had even moved her fingers but he said, "Good."

Her lips formed a dry whisper, "My head hurts."

"Yes," he said, and chuckled as if delighted. "We'll give you something for the pain."

She was completely disoriented. Who was talking to her? Why was she floating in and out of a nothingness that was without time and feeling?

The next time when she was able to keep her eyes open for more than a minute, she asked, "Where am I?"

"You're in a hospital," a familiar voice told her.

She slowly turned her head. Scott? She blinked to keep his face in focus.

"Hi, sleepyhead." Bending over her, he gave her a smile that eased the tension lines around his mouth. "Time to wake up."

She frowned. "How long have I been asleep?"

He chuckled. "Only two weeks. You took a nice long nap. The doctor says you're doing great. You'll be out of here in no time, and just as stubborn and ornery as ever."

As he talked, bits and pieces of memory floated back, but her foggy brain refused to sort them out. "What happened? How did I get here?"

Scott shook his head. "Honey, those two questions alone could take the better part of the day to answer. I'll explain everything later after you're stronger. I have lots of things to tell you, but you have to rest now."

She saw that tired lines creased his face, his cheeks looked hollow and a five-o'clock shadow darkened his complexion. "You look awful."

"Just like a woman," he chided with a grin. "She scares the daylights out of a man and then finds fault because he hasn't shaved." He bent his head and kissed her lightly on the lips.

"That was nice," she said, liking the way he was looking at her. She raised a weak hand and brushed hair back from his forehead.

Her loving touch made him resolve once again that whatever it took to get her well and happy again, he was determined to see that nothing got in the way—not even himself. This was one time in his life when he wasn't going to be selfish about what he wanted, but do what was best for her, even if it meant a new heartache for himself.

Chapter Fifteen

Allie's recovery was rapid, but the doctor kept her in the hospital a few extra days to make certain that there were no complications. She was sitting in a wheelchair, enjoying the hospital's sun porch when Peggy Crawford brought Cathy and Randy to see her.

Both of the children were carrying small bouquets of flowers. Cathy was dressed in a perky little sundress and had yellow ribbons in her curly hair. Randy wore a pair of new jeans and a T-shirt that read "Cool Cat." His hair had been cut into one of those modern boyish styles that Allie secretly found amusing.

Allie smiled when she saw them. They certainly didn't look like the two ragamuffin children who had slept under a rock ledge, hiked miles in a drenching rain and fled across slippery rocks in a mountain stream. She remembered how she had tucked them in at night and heard their prayers. She doubted if many adults could have lived up to their undaunted spirits. What a blessing that they had adapted to the changes and challenges with the open trust of children who lived in the moment. How grateful she was that they were brought home safe and sound. If anyone had to get hurt, she was glad it was she. If she hadn't reacted as quickly as she did, it might have been Cathy who would have fallen down the hillside.

"We've had a hard time keeping them away," Peggy said. "We called the hospital every day to see how you were doing, but we didn't want to come and tire you out. I think they would have camped out on the hospital steps if we would have let them."

Allie laughed, thanked them for the flowers and gave them to a nurse to put in water. Then she held out her arms. "How about a hug, you two?"

Cathy rushed to her, but Randy held back, eyeing the bandage wrapped around her head and what remained of her close-cropped hair.

Allie winked at him. "I look pretty funny, huh?"

"Kinda. But not *too* funny," the boy added quickly as if he didn't want to hurt her feelings.

Cathy was wearing her hearing aids so she echoed Randy's words, "Not too funny."

Allie smiled to herself. As always, Cathy was still following Randy's lead. They were kindred spirits who had found themselves outside the norm—Cathy because of her hearing loss, and Randy because of his deprived background. From the beginning they had paired up against the world. It was obvious that the traumatic experiences they'd shared had only made the bond between them even stronger.

"I guess you hurt your head, huh?" Randy said, frowning. "They said you were in something like... like a comma."

"Not a comma, a coma," Allie said, suppressing a smile. "A coma is a deep sleep, but I'm wide-awake now. And my head is going to be as good as new. My hair will grow out, and I'll look just the way I did before."

As Randy's frown eased into a boyish smile, she realized that he had been worried about her. His tough little exterior didn't go very deep. She knew how tender and sensitive he could be, and she wondered how he was making out with his foster parents. His relationship with them had been rocky from the start, and Allie only hoped that the flood ordeal had helped smooth out some of the friction between them. She hated to think about his being shifted to another foster home so soon.

"Thank the dear Lord, you're going to be all right," Peggy said, her eyes growing misty. "We're terribly grateful to you and Mr. Davidson for all you did. I was hoping to thank him again in person. Randy talks about him all the time."

"Scott's been spending a lot of time here at the hospital, but at the moment, he's in California." Allie kept a smile on her face, but deep inside she felt a sudden sadness.

When Scott had left her the day before, she knew that their parting was inevitable. For more than two weeks he'd put aside all obligations to be with her, but now that she was well on the road to recovery, and would be released in a few days, there was no reason for him to put off picking up his life again. He was obviously anxious about his business, and everything that had been put on hold. She knew he had been trying to take care of business by telephone.

"When's he coming back?" Randy asked with his usual bluntness.

She moistened her lips. "I don't know."

Scott had been vague about how much time it would take to get his business back in shape. She knew his mother was on the phone to him daily, urging him to come home as quickly as possible. He promised to call Allie every evening, and she knew it was foolish to mark the hours until she heard his voice again, but she couldn't help herself. She didn't doubt for a minute that Randy and Cathy were missing him. "I'll tell him you asked about him, Randy," she promised.

"I ain't going back to that foster place," Randy announced with the air of someone who had made a decision and was ready to fight off her objections.

"What?" She was at a loss for a moment as to how to deal with his childish declaration.

"I ain't gonna live with them no more."

Peggy Crawford laughed, and gave him an affectionate pat on his shoulder. "That's right. Randy's going to be our little boy now. We're adopting him."

"Me, too," said Cathy. "I 'dopt him for my brother."

For a moment Allie thought she must still be in some kind of a hallucinating fog, but the nodding smiles of the two children made her realize she wasn't dreaming. Overcome by a swell of emotion that put tears in her own eyes, Allie could only stammer, "That's...that's...wonderful."

"We think so, too," Peggy said happily. "We've always wanted a son, and now we have one who's been hand-picked by our daughter. We expect some challenges," she said with a knowing smile at Allie, "but I know that Randy will be happy with us, and having a home will make up for a lot of things."

"You'll come see us, Allie?" Cathy asked.

"Sure she will," Randy answered for her. "I've got my own room and everything. Even a radio!" he added with such fervor that Allie broke out laughing. How could she ever forget all the tests of patience that he had put them through, just being Randy?

She hugged and kissed them when they got ready to leave, thankful that these two precious children would always be a special part of her life. She promised that she'd come to see them as soon as she was on her feet again.

After they'd gone, she went back to her room, and tried to dispel a feeling of despondency as she lay there looking at the ceiling. Tears threatened to spill down her cheeks despite an inner voice that reminded her how lucky she was. If it hadn't been for the miracles of the scrub oak bushes breaking her fall, and the circling of eagles overhead to draw attention to the high meadow, she could have died. Even as she breathed prayers of thankfulness, a sense of loss remained, and as she looked at the telephone, wishing it would ring, she knew why her heart felt so heavy.

During her hospital stay, her school friends and church people had sent dozens of cards wishing her a quick recovery. Reverend Hanson had made daily visits and she'd found his quiet serenity a haven of peace and security as they talked and prayed together.

The doctor had discouraged visitors while Allie was still under strong medication for the pain in her head, but now that she was almost herself again, the word had gone out that she was ready to see some of her friends.

Her spirits rose when she woke up from a nap, and discovered she had two more visitors waiting to see her. Patrick and Dorie came into her room with broad smiles on their faces. They looked well, and Allie had tears in her eyes as they came over to her bed. Remembering how worried she'd been about them, she blubbered. "How wonderful to see you! Did you get flooded out?" Allie asked, wondering if their lovely little home had met the same fate as the camp buildings.

"Nope," said Patrick. "Thank the Lord our place was on higher ground, and we were one of the lucky ones. There were plenty of families up and down the river that lost everything."

"Trudy told us a little bit about your narrow escape when the bridge went out," Dorie said with a shiver. "Sure and it chills my heart to think of you and the little ones out in that horrible storm."

"It was a bad time, not knowing," Patrick agreed. "From what Trudy said, I guess you were holed up in the Thompsons' place until the mudslides started."

Allie leaned forward. At last she was going to know something about the couple who had been in her thoughts for so long. "Is that their name?"

He nodded. "Jim and Ruth Thompson. That place has been in their family for a long time, and they've been fixing it up for several summers now. Just had a baby this last year."

"We could tell there was a baby. And we knew someone had given a lot of tender, loving care to the place. The lower road was already under water when we managed to get to the cabin. The place was empty." Allie knew she had to ask the horrible question that had taunted her all the time they'd stayed in the cabin. "What happened to them? It looked as if they might have just left...and got caught in the flood waters."

Patrick shook his head. "I heard they were in town getting supplies, and decided to spend the night with some friends before going back to their place in the morning. They were roused out of bed like the rest of us, but were safe enough."

"That's wonderful! I'll bet if they walked through the door I'd know who they were. They must have been surprised to find squatters had used their home while they were gone," Allie said. "They had a broken window to repair and most of their foodstuffs were gone from the pantry. I didn't have time to even straighten up before the slides sent us running for our lives. We'll get their address and send them some money to make things even."

"Don't you be worrying your head about it. There are some lessons to be learned out of a disaster. People are ready to help others, share what they have and give of themselves wherever they can. Hundreds of volunteers are working on the clean-up."

"There's nothing left of Rainbow Camp," Dorie said sadly. "From what I hear, Scott's buyers still want the property. Rumors are that they're going to put condos higher on the hillside, away from any danger of a flood like this one."

Now she knew why Scott was anxious to get back to taking care of business. It wasn't so much the sale

of his father's property that saddened her, but the fact
that he couldn't wait to finalize the deal.

"So he's going ahead with the sale," Allie said
with a catch in her throat.

"Yep, sure looks like it," Patrick said. "Some out-
fit is already busy building a new bridge and clearing
everything away."

"You can't even tell where the camp used to be,"
Dorie lamented.

"Now woman, don't go on teary," chided Patrick.
"This little lady has enough to think about. We just
have to 'let go, and let God' do His work. No use
looking backward."

No use looking backward. Patrick's words lingered
long after they'd left.

When Trudy came to see her later in the day, Allie
told her about the O'Tooles' visit, and the good news
about Randy.

"Who says that good things don't come out of
bad?" Trudy bubbled. "I could tell at the camp that
there was a special bond between those two kids.
He'll be a great older brother. Funny how things work
out," she mused. "Just like you and Scott being
thrown together like that." She eyed Allie, obviously
wanting Allie to elaborate.

"Trudy, you're as transparent as a piece of glass,"
Allie chided.

"And you're as closemouthed as anybody I've ever
known. Come on, give a little. Even Scott is more
forthcoming with a little information that you are.
He's crazy about you, I can tell that."

"He told you that?"

"Not in so many words," Trudy admitted. "But

for Pete's sake, Allie, the guy's been hanging out here day and night, sleeping on that hard waiting-room sofa and jumping every time a nurse went in and out of your room. Anyone with two eyes in his head can see where he's coming from."

"That's the problem, Trudy, I know where he's coming from. And I don't want to go there."

"And where is that?"

"You know the answer to that. You saw and heard what kinds of things were important to him. I don't think you even liked him."

"He doesn't seem like the same guy now. I think he's changed."

"For how long? Let's be honest. The kind of traumatic experience we had could put anyone momentarily off balance. His normal perspective on life might have been shaken, temporarily, but at the core of his being, Scott is still focused on his business and his chosen lifestyle."

"But you're in love with the guy. I know you are. All the time we were at camp, you were practically wearing your heart on your sleeve."

"I was caught up in what used to be. First love, and all that," she admitted. "And being with him during the flood reminded me of all his wonderful qualities. No one could have sacrificed himself more to keep us safe than he did. In some ways we were able to get to know each other on many different levels, both positive and negative."

"Don't you think that sometimes love returns to give slow learners a second chance?" Trudy teased.

"Perhaps," Allie conceded. "If the important things haven't changed. But we can't make people into what we think they should be. I want a spiritually-centered life, and I want a partner to share it with me. As much as I love Scott, and, yes, I do love him," she admitted, "we don't look at life the same way."

"Well, I don't think it would do any harm for you to give the guy a little slack and see what happens." She winked at Allie. "Sometimes, you're a little hardnosed for my taste. But I love you anyway." She bent over the bed and gave Allie a kiss on the cheek.

After she'd gone, Allie thought about their conversation, and wondered if Trudy was right. Was she being too rigid about her convictions? Was her dedication to living a life she felt was in harmony with faith and trust in God too narrow for today's world? She closed her eyes and prayed for guidance.

When Scott called her that night, those questions were still nagging at her. Just hearing the sound of his voice sent warmth sluicing through her body. He'd only been gone a couple of days, and it had seemed like twenty.

"How you doing, sweetheart?"

Her pulse quickened at the endearment. "I'm doing fine. The doctor just left and he said I could go home the day after tomorrow. They want to do a bunch of tests before they release me, but he thinks the picture of my head is going to be okay."

"So soon? I mean, I'd hoped to be able to get away from here in time to take you home."

"No problem," she said, hiding the disappointment. "Trudy plans on staying with me a few days, anyway, so she'll see me home." She moistened her lips. "How are things at your end?" He didn't answer and after a prolonged silence, she said softly, "That bad, huh?"

"I won't bore you with the details."

She could hear the stress in his voice. She knew that staying in Colorado as long as he had had not been to his choosing. More than once, he'd expressed a concern for what was happening in the California office. Obviously, things had been worse than he'd expected.

"I'm sorry," she said, "but I bet you'll get a handle on things in short order."

"It's going to take some time. I don't see how I can be away again for very long." He paused. "I was wondering how you'd feel about coming to California and spending the rest of the summer recuperating in our beach house. Plenty of sun and relaxation. It'd be great for you."

"I don't know," she hedged, at once drawn to the idea and yet disturbed by the suggestion.

His voice softened. "Frankly I'm having withdrawal symptoms. Since it's going to be hard for me to get back to Colorado, it would be great if you could come out here. I could get away from the city on weekends."

"Just weekends?"

"Unfortunately, the distance is too great for daily commuting, and I can't take any more time off until I get things straightened out. I've got some big issues hanging."

She could picture the furrows in his brow and the firm set of his mouth. In spite of everything that had happened to them, in spite of the miracles that had kept them safe and brought them to safety, the corporate Scott Davidson was back. It would be foolish to pretend that he'd changed from the hard-driving realist who had made gods out of money and earthly power. Cold, worldly reality had claimed him again.

"Please come, Allie. We need some time together when we're not trying to outrun mudslides and climbing mountains in the rain. I should have told you how I feel about you, how much I want you in my life."

"Don't, Scott," she said with a catch in her throat. She didn't want to hear him say he loved her. The kind of love she wanted and needed in her life had to be based on more than romantic attraction. She wanted to share a mystical, spiritual love that came from the soul—not a bank account.

His voice became a blur in her ears as he talked. Her heart was full of so many things she wanted to say, but couldn't. The distance between them was more than just miles. If he'd asked her to marry him, there was only one answer she could have given him.

After he'd hung up, she very slowly returned the receiver to its cradle, and whispered, "Goodbye, Scott."

Chapter Sixteen

As planned, Trudy came to the hospital when Allie was released. After sharing her profusion of flower bouquets and plants with others, Allie bid everyone goodbye, and thanked the staff for the wonderful care they had given her.

The joy that Allie felt when they pulled into the driveway of her modest home was greater than any homecoming she'd ever experienced. Never had the small white bungalow looked more beautiful. The neighborhood was an old one with tall oak trees and family homes. Several of her neighbors came rushing over even before she'd gotten out of the car. They poured out best wishes and promises to bring food over now that they knew she was home.

"Someone's been cutting your lawn and watering your flowers," Trudy remarked as they walked to the front door.

"I wonder who," Allie mused.

"Beats me," Trudy answered with a sly smile that

gave her away. "I think you'll find all the plants in the house still alive—except for that funny looking feathery plant in the kitchen. It looks like a wet mop."

"Over-watering will do that," Allie said kindly. "It'll dry out. Thanks, Trudy. You're an angel."

"Oh, sure." Trudy gave a dismissing wave of her hand. "I have wings and a halo that I rent out by the hour."

Laughing, they went into the house, and as Allie walked through the rooms, she knew that she'd never take all the treasures of her life for granted again. She smiled as she touched her favorite pillow, listened to the chimes of the old clock that had been her mother's, and gazed at a drawing that one of her students had given her, signed, "To Miss Allie with Love."

She refused to go to bed as Trudy suggested, and sat down on the living room sofa. "I've had enough bed, thank you."

Trudy opened her mouth to protest, but seeing Allie's stubborn look, she nodded. "All right, then sit, and I'll bring you a cup of tea."

A few minutes later, she carried Allie's favorite tea set, and some freshly baked muffins in on a tray. "I came over early and put them in the oven before I went after you. I wanted to make sure you had a happy homecoming." Then she eyed Allie. "Which reminds me, what about Scott? I half expected him to show up at the hospital today. Is he still calling you?"

Allie took a sip of tea before answering. "Yes. We talk every night."

"And?" Trudy raised a questioning eyebrow.

"There's no 'and,'" Allie answered in a flat tone. "Scott is as busy as ever, maybe even busier. I think he's trying to make up for lost time. Anyway, even though we talk about our time together, I don't have the feeling that much has changed since the day he agreed to let us have church camp."

"Do you think he loves you?"

"In his way."

"Maybe you should go to California and—"

"And what, Trudy? Scott and I spent many hours together, depending upon each other for survival, and sharing what was in our hearts under the most intimate circumstances. He was up-front with me then about his lack of faith in God, and he's never said anything to me that makes me think he's changed his mind. Undoubtedly he would be a good husband and father for someone who looks at life the same way, and wants the same things. I know I couldn't be happy or make him happy, even though—" She faltered.

"Even though you're in love with the guy?" Trudy finished.

Allie didn't answer but reached for another muffin. "These are very good," she said in an attempt to change the subject.

"It seems to me your faith is a little ragged at the edges, Allie. Why don't you—" She broke off as the doorbell rang, and sent Allie an "I told you so" look. Then she hurried out of the living room into the hall.

Allie stiffened as she heard the door open. Was it Scott? Had he come, after all? Her heartbeat quickened, and her chest suddenly felt tight with anticipation. She held her breath, but the hopeful moment passed when she recognized the voices of Randy and Cathy.

"Look who I have here," Trudy said, smiling as she came in with the two children. "Peggy Crawford dropped them off for a short visit. I told her I'd run them home when I saw you getting tired." There was a warning in her voice that Allie wasn't supposed to make the visit a long one.

After hugs all around, Randy cocked his head to one side and studied the almost healed wound on Allie's head. "How many stitches?"

"Twenty-five."

"Bummer, that's a lot. Some creep I knew had only six when he got hit in the head with a bottle."

Allie wasn't about to pursue that line of conversation. She suspected that Randy might not have been an innocent bystander to the bottle throwing. She smiled at Cathy. "Is your big brother behaving himself?"

"Pretty good," Cathy said rather cautiously, and then quickly added, "He's awful smart."

Randy beamed and answered her with some quick hand signs, and she giggled. "He's funny, too."

"Would you kids like a muffin and some milk?" Trudy asked. They both nodded. "I put a few things in the fridge for you, Allie. You can make out a list and I'll run to the store for you."

Trudy started toward the kitchen, but was stopped by the doorbell. She frowned. "Probably one of the neighbors. I think we're going to have to put a stop to all this visiting. They can leave the food and come back tomorrow or the next day to see you.'' The next moment Trudy was back with a huge fruit basket in her arms. ''Guess what?''

Allie didn't even hear what Trudy was saying. Her eyes were fastened on the giver of the basket who was coming into the room behind Trudy with a smile on his face.

''Surprise,'' Scott said with a boyish grin. ''I would have made it to the hospital before you left, but my plane was late.''

Allie didn't have a chance to answer him as Randy's face broke in a wide smile, and Cathy ran into his arms, squealing, ''Scott.''

He swung her up and made a twirl in the middle of the living room, while the little girl laughed and squealed. When he put her down, he reached out and hugged Randy. ''How you doing, big fellow? I hear you got yourself a brand-new family?''

''I'm a Crawford, now,'' he bragged. ''Randy Crawford.''

''Sounds like a winner to me. And that's some haircut!'' He winked at Allie.

She smiled back, a sudden warmth easing away all tiredness. In appearance Scott looked very much like the polished young businessman who had answered the door when she'd come to the house to convince him not to cancel the church camp. He was dressed in the same kind of expensive attire, chambray open-neck shirt, matching trousers and sports coat in shades of blue-gray. His dark hair was layered in a stylish cut that accented his tanned face and neck. Success and prosperity were written all over him, but in her heart, Allie preferred the mud-soaked, bedraggled Scott, wearing grimy clothes, and shocks of wet hair dripping down his face.

Allie felt Trudy's eyes upon her, searching her expression, and she hoped that the wild beating of her heart wasn't evident in her suddenly heated face. Watching Scott and the children, she was swept back in her mind's eye to that small summer cabin when every moment had been a precious one because they were safe, and together. She hadn't known it then, but that was pure happiness, the kind that surpasses all understanding.

"I was about to serve some milk and muffins. Would you like one with a cup of tea, Scott?" Trudy asked.

"Sounds great. I'm especially fond of hot tea." His eyes met Allie's. Scott couldn't tell what her reaction was to his sudden appearance. Did she remember how they had sat together in that small kitchen, hugging warm mugs of tea in their chilled hands? There was something in her manner that warned him not to take her in his arms and hold her close, so he stood rather awkwardly in the middle of the floor with the children hanging on him.

Trudy picked up the teapot. "I'll heat this up and get some more muffins. Come on, kids, you can help me." She herded them into the kitchen ahead of her.

"Have a seat, Scott," Allie said politely.

He sat down in a chair opposite the sofa. He couldn't tell whether Allie was just surprised to see him or his presence disturbed her. He'd felt a great chasm open up between them during her hospital stay. Even though he telephoned every night, the silence on her end of the line was like a closed door. She seemed to be warning him not to mistake what had happened between them to be an invitation into her life.

There was so much he wanted to say, but didn't have a clue where to begin. Maybe he shouldn't have come to Denver her first day out of the hospital, but he couldn't wait. There were too many things he wanted settled between them. "How are you doing?" he asked lamely.

"I'm nearly a hundred percent okay," she assured him. "I don't know why I had to stay in the hospital as long as I did." She smiled at him. "I had a florist shop to give away this morning. Is there any kind of flower you didn't send?" she teased.

"I couldn't think of anything else that would tell you how much I was thinking about you, wanting to be with you and needing reassurance that you were going to be as feisty and stubborn as always." If she only knew how many hours he'd spent wishing he could get on the next plane to Colorado, but there were things he had to do that couldn't be hurried, and he had no choice but to stay and see them through.

"And how have you been?" she asked politely, torn between the need to hear how he felt about her, and yet afraid that it would only make it harder to keep her feelings in check. "You look great. Nice tan."

"I have a pool and swim every day. It's a good way to relax." He gave her a wry smile.

A swimming pool. Of course, all prosperous Californians had their own swimming pools. Her heart sank. She could just imagine the expensive house he called home. He'd hinted once that it was a good investment in California real estate. They talked a few minutes like strangers until Trudy and the children came back. Instantly the situation lightened.

It was obvious to Allie that Cathy and Randy had no trouble accepting Scott as the same guy who had led them through the rain, washed their clothes, painted a sign for the roof and brought them home in a helicopter. They loved and trusted him, and Allie saw Scott begin to relax and enjoy himself. She was glad the children were there to break the ice.

"Well, I think I'd better run these kids home," Trudy said after they'd finished their snack. With a knowing nod at Allie, she added, "I'm sure you two have a few things to talk about." Then she turned to Scott. "I don't suppose you came all the way from California just to have a cup of tea and a muffin, did you?"

"Now that you mention it, I did have a couple of more things on my mind." Smiling, he reached out and shook her hand. He remembered all the hours they'd spent at the hospital waiting for the doctors and nurses to give them some news of Allie's condition. "Thanks for being there for Allie."

She winked at him. "I should be gone about an hour, if you get what I mean."

Allie flushed. "Trudy, don't be so obvious."

"Why not? Somebody around here ought to call things as they are."

She herded the children out of the room, and both Allie and Scott laughed at the punctuating bang she gave the front door.

He searched Allie's face for a long moment. "Well, if I only have an hour, I'd better make good use of it."

Without waiting for an invitation, he came over and sat beside Allie on the sofa. "I've missed you," he said softly. "There are times when I wished we were still sitting in front of the fire, listening to rain patter on the roof."

"Me, too," she admitted.

He put an arm around her shoulder, and gently pulled her closer. Although he'd held her hand when she was still in the hospital, there had been no chance for any more closeness. "We have to talk. And I don't mean one of those insipid telephone conversations, either."

"Scott, I don't think this is a good time." The feel of his arm around her, and the wonderful warmth of his nearness was too much for her to handle on any rational level.

"Are you too tired?" he asked, searching her face anxiously.

"No, it's not that. It's just…just that I don't feel like talking," she finished lamely.

"That's okay, honey. I'll do the talking." He leaned his head against hers for a long moment, and then straightened up, still keeping his arm around her shoulders. "You've probably guessed that I had my hands full when I went back home. I thought I could get everything whipped into shape and get back here, but there were a million details to take care of. I never knew that selling a business could be so exasperating.''

At first the words didn't register, and when they did, she drew in a quick breath. ''What? You're selling your business?''

''Didn't you believe me when I promised to get back to Colorado as soon as I could?''

''I thought you meant for a visit. I didn't know you were planning on moving back.''

His voice softened. ''When I left you in the hospital, knowing you were going to be all right, I knew that I'd been given another chance to make things right in my life. I don't expect you to believe me just because I say so, but I intend to prove to you that I'm back on the right track now. All those spiritual values that were important when I was young have deeper meaning for me now—kind of like the prodigal son returning, I guess,'' he said earnestly.

''Oh, Scott, are you sure?'' Hope leaped like a geyser. Was he telling the truth that he had been healed of his anger toward the Almighty and was ready to renew his faith and belief in God's love and protection?

''Yes, I'm sure.'' He didn't know how to explain that when he'd prayed up there on that mountain for the Lord to save her, nothing else in his life had mattered then—or now. He tenderly lifted her chin and looked steadily into her shining eyes. ''I love you so much, Allie. Please give me a chance to share your life. If you'll marry me, I promise to make you happy.''

Without hesitation, she lifted her lips to his, and her answer was clear and sure. Love that had blossomed a long time ago now sprang full bloom. "Yes...yes...yes," she answered, smiling at him.

"And there's one other thing," he murmured. "I'm not selling the property. I've decided to keep it."

She searched his eyes and saw a glint of excitement there that sent hope surging through her. "Why?"

"Well, since I'll be setting up my business in Denver, there will be time to oversee the building of a new Rainbow Camp—higher on the mountainside, of course. In fact, I already have a set of plans drawn up for some modern cabins, and a spacious lodge. There's only one thing I haven't decided on. I was waiting for you to choose the plans for your mountain home."

"How did you know I was going to say 'yes' to your proposal?"

He kissed her playfully on the tip of her nose. "I didn't, but with God on my side, how could you refuse?"

* * * * *

Dear Readers,

I have chosen the grandeur of the Rocky Mountains as the setting for my story of love, danger and inspiration, because as a native of Colorado, my life has been enriched by God's magnificent panorama of high, snow-tipped peaks, rushing mountain streams and green-carpeted hillsides. Sitting quietly and breathing in the high clear air, my spirit rises to touch the heavens. It is a joy to share this part of my spiritual life with my readers.

The books I enjoy reading the most are exciting page-turners about people who are like you and me. My goal is to write that kind of book. Happily, my characters move in with me when I'm writing their story, and I hope that they will find a place in your heart, too. The lesson they learn is one for all of us—it is never too late to make a U-turn and get back on the path the Lord has laid out for us.

Please enjoy.

Leona Karr

Next Month
From Steeple Hill's

Love Inspired®

A HERO FOR KELSEY
by
Carolyne Aarsen

*After her husband died and left her and her
young son with nothing, Kelsey Swain found
herself working at her parents' diner. When her
husband's best friend, Will Dempsey, steps in to
lend a hand, an undeniable attraction between
them grows. But can Will convince her that
heroes really do exist?*

**Don't miss
A HERO FOR KELSEY
On sale April 2001**

Available at your favorite retail outlet.

 *Love Inspired*®

Visit us at www.steeplehill.com   LIAHFK

Next Month From Steeple Hill's

Love Inspired®

COURTING KATARINA

by

Carol Steward

THE SEQUEL TO
SECOND TIME AROUND

Katarina Berthoff and Alex MacIntyre meet at the wedding of her sister and his brother—and sparks start to fly! But the beautiful dollmaker has a fear of commitment, and the rugged forest firefighter is ready to settle down and raise a family. Discover how Alex convinces Kat that they're truly meant to be together.

**Don't miss
COURTING KATARINA
On sale April 2001**

Available at your favorite retail outlet.

Love Inspired®

Visit us at www.steeplehill.com   LICK

Next Month From Steeple Hill's

Love Inspired®

THE MARRYING KIND
by

Cynthia Rutledge

An important business merger is threatened by an impossible ultimatum: Nick Lanagan must date the boss's daughter or no deal! Nick desperately enlists the lovely Taylor Rollins into a pretend engagement to save the deal. Smart, beautiful and faithful to the Lord, Taylor is everything a man could want. Suddenly Nick is struggling to keep their engagement purely professional.

**Don't miss
THE MARRYING KIND
On sale April 2001**

Available at your favorite retail outlet.

Love Inspired®

Visit us at www.steeplehill.com   LITMK